*The Gita
and
Management*

The Gita
and
Management

Swami Bodhananda

BLUEJAY BOOKS

An imprint of Srishti Publishers & Distributors
New Delhi & Calcutta

BLUEJAY BOOKS
An imprint of SRISHTI PUBLISHERS & DISTRIBUTORS
64-A, Adhchini
Sri Aurobindo Marg
New Delhi 110 017

First published by Sambodh Foundation in 1994
This revised edition published by *B L U E J A Y B O O K S* 2003
Reprinted 2004

©Sambodh Foundation

ISBN 81-88575-09-7
Rs. 195.00

Cover Ganesha: P. Khemraj
Etching/Engraving, Fishes Guild: Nirmal Parkash
Cover design by Creative Concept

Typeset in AGaramond 11 pt. by Skumar at Srishti

Printed and bound in India by
Saurabh Printers Pvt. Ltd., Noida

This edition is only for sale in India, Pakistan, Srilanka, Bangladesh
and Nepal

Ancient Wisdom

Swami Bodhananda's teachings, meditation techniques and value systems, are based on his deep study of eastern mysticism and spiritual traditioins, especially of the *Vedas*, the *Upanishads*, the especially *Gita* and the life and works of saints like Adi Sankaracharya, Ramkrishna Paramahasana, Ramana Maharishi, Sri Aurobindo, and from his own deep mystical experience.

His teachings are a powerful combination of ancient wisdom and modern scholarship, meshed in the crucible of his own long years of *sadhana* and unique spiritual insights.

Creativity

In our search for creative energy, for tackling myriad complex problems, we are increasingly turning to inner resources and strength – of intuition, of psychic energy, cosmic intelligence, spontaneity, and harmonious field energies. Creativity is an expression of a silent, alert, aware, attentive, open mind, functioning without an ego centre – the Me.

How do we attain that mental state of supreme dynamism and natural creativity? Meditate, says Swamiji.

Foreword

Every literary work is a reflection of the times in which it is written and provides a vision of future realities. However, every literary work does not leave the reader there. It goes beyond. It attempts to provide a coherent moral attitude. This book, like all creative writing, has a dual significance both for the individual and for society at large. It serves to prepare the minds of people for the new age – the age of information explosion. The issues raised, and thoughts expressed by Swamiji in this book, are an attempt to prepare our minds for this new age.

Swamiji's talks, interpreting the concepts of management with reference to the *Bhagavad Gita*, guide us toward creative destruction. We are still clinging to much that is dead and needs to be discarded. To discard intelligently we need inner strength. Hence, we must consciously reinforce and nurture the constructive forces and phase out the disruptive ones. We have to evolve an intelligent approach to dealing with the major and minor issues of life. We need to harness the constructive forces within us to stay focused and integrated. This requires both positive thinking and a creative approach not only in one's personal life but at the work place as well.

Swamiji reminds us that society rises to a higher level not through mechanical or technological efficiency but by practising sound moral and ethical values. The driving, re-engineering and reviving forces come from within. In fact, scientific advances are also the outcome of union with the perfect Supreme Intelligent Being. God is *satyasvarupa*. Every scientific discovery, too, is one more *svarupa* of God so why reject the basic values and traditions espoused in our scriptures?

Swamiji's observations, both incisive, and at times even provocative, on issues of creativity and positive thinking, compel the reader to undertake self-analysis; transcend the obvious limitations and dilemmas of life, and look to the future with hope and certainty. He exhorts us not to seek to revolutionise societies but, instead, to look for creative solutions which are more nourishing and sustaining.

By referring to the *Bhagavad Gita* and the holy scriptures, Swamiji is not evoking religious thinking *per se*, but guiding the reader gently to go beyond the frailties of human life. In this respect, the reference to religious texts is simply to stress that the presence of God is immanent in every activity of life: mundane, domestic and scientific research. This intrinsic religion should find expression in our work and in every activity of life.

In the introductory chapter, Swamiji has commented on the nature of work and the five factors which go into the execution of work. They are the ego, the physical and mental faculties, inbuilt values and external forces. When one works in a way which harmonises all these factors, the work becomes enjoyable. The worker becomes self-motivated. On the other hand, people become restless without work. Therefore, work should be viewed as a positive activity.

This book speaks of three types of work: *karma,* individual work; *dharma,* group-oriented work; *yajna karma,* group-oriented work which is egoless and dedicated. This is the ideal view of work. At this stage methodologies for observing *svadharma* are not clearly spelt out. The reader is left with the thought to be positively disposed to all external influences in order to lead a wholesome competitive coexistence in this world.

In the same vein, "Spiritual Dimensions in Modern Management" proceeds to guide the reader to incorporate spirituality in his work-life and in his personal life. The thoughts do not focus on traditional and orthodox values and visions of religious rituals but on techniques by which one can become an effective competitor in the world market. The spiritual dimension refers to the revival of inner strength, which is a sensitivity that can be felt and experienced but not measured. This prepares an individual to cope with the environmental scramble and existential stress. Revival of the spiritual dimension enables an individual to become a naturally happy person with no real gap between his public and private face. Such a person is a realised person because he looks for inspiration and strength within himself. This is a feature which is possible not only for managers but for all individuals every where.

Swamiji, thus, is speaking on a wide canvas which is the

world at large. He exhorts the reader to function like an intelligent person by pooling resources and maximising them through team-work. The pooled output is likely to lead to a higher ideal and to generate greater manifestation of energy and enthusiasm. Thus, the seeds of a better work-culture are sown in this chapter. The picture before us is of an ideal, beautiful world. The question is: Is it possible to create such a world? Perhaps the answer lies in the basic nature of man, which is one of striving toward the attainment of excellence.

One approach to intelligent management suggested by Swamiji, is positive thinking. The dilemma is evident in so many intelligent economic schemes being launched in our world. Does positive thinking have to be consciously cultivated? Perhaps it is so because many a cherished philosophy has failed to satisfy either the poor or the middle class or even the rich! Therefore, conscious cultivation and nurturing of a positive attitude where one feels that "I can do" rather than "Can I do?" is imperative. The significant aspects of this positive thinking is clarity about the goal and playing a positive supportive role for those who seek our help and guidance. Creativity means pro-activity. We have to try to invoke this attitude from within by reinforcing the spiritual dimension which was discussed earlier.

In this entire scheme of things, Swamiji has stressed the role of the individual. The central concern of all managers should be the individual and successful enterprises are those which are highly people-sensitive and people-centred. Then only will the organisation give work to people which not only enhances their self-worth but also gives them the joy of working. Such persons become inspired workers. Their inspiration is derived from spiritual strength and reinforced by positive thinking. This is an idealist's view of life which needs to be debated further and in greater depth.

Swamiji further enlightens us on the subject of motivating and inspiring the worker by drawing upon the wisdom in the *Bhagavad Gita*. He advises us to begin on a positive note in our perceptions of those who seek to work with us. The starting point is to look at another person with the eye of friendliness. The reason is that both manager and worker are in a common enterprise and therefore both must work together productively in every aspect of organisational life. The same approach holds true in our personal life as well. Thus to make an overall success of our lives, an attitudinal shift is recommended. Then only does work become a means of unfolding collective creative energies rather than a mere economic activity. This is, no doubt, a very compelling idea. These attitudes can become a concrete reality only when they arise from within and are not imposed from without.

One's mind is at times clouded with questions like "Can I become a natural worker as suggested?" In response to this and other doubts, the last section, the question-answer sessions, makes very relevant reading.

It covers a wide range of issues including the acceptance of such idealism by the poor majority in India who are basically preoccupied with the stress of daily living. Swamiji responds to each of these questions with characteristic humour and candidness. What comes to the fore is his sustained optimism, which alone lends hope for the future generations.

The world of work today is full of stress and strife. Therefore, reliance on one's physical competencies is never sufficient. We have to draw upon inner strength. Reviving the spiritual dimension has become imperative for modern Man. This book provides a workable philosophy for revival of inner strength so that one can lead a creative life and fulfilled existence. One can thus become a high-quality individual. Logically such high-quality individuals are most likely to become high-quality managers and help organisations to become temples of work. The onus to realise these potentialities is on us, without losing sight of the reality that we can reorganise some part of society, but not all of it. Some deficiencies will remain, but some changes can be made. Towards such an evolution this book is a significant contribution.

Dr. Meena Kishore

Introduction

It is an incontrovertible fact that modern management theory and practice lay great stress on people as 'workers' and 'consumers', representing two aspects of management concerns. This is reflected in sayings like, "Workers are the greatest resource", "Consumer is King", etc. The main management problems are how to motivate workers to perform optimally, how to organise their recruitment and training, and how to satisfy the customer. This might include how to inspire him to buy a product and how to identify and respond innovatively to his needs in terms of products. The questions management science grapples with are two-fold – to motivate workers and inspire consumers. Man is the focus of attention. Money, technology and organisational structures are all subservient to human nature and need. Therefore, the key lies in understanding humans. Psychology, anthropology, sociology and the other behavioural sciences have all sought to study man as the centre of economic relationships. Even then, human behaviour, whether as individuals or groups, remains most unpredictable. Man is surely an enigma.

Individual and group behaviour with reference to productive and consumptive activities varies from culture to culture, country to country and group to group, depending upon the historical origins, traditions and life situations of peoples. Thus the work culture of America is different from that of India. The consumption needs of the people of Europe are different from those of Africa. But as the world becomes smaller and more integrated through communication networks enabled by information technology, goods and people travel faster, and almost a quarter of the world's population has become global in its outlook, values, habits and needs. Gradually but steadily, the rest will be moving into that bracket. Substantial differences, however, still exist between the workforces of different countries and consumption needs of people due to climatic, cultural, and economic differences.

Management science has to take this factor into account while formulating theories and ideas for different societies. That is why American, European and Japanese management practices exhibit such distinct characteristics. If the American management style is thoroughly contractual, on a hire-and-fire basis, Europeans have a dash of family and patriotic values thrown in while in Japan complete job security and pride in the company's honour govern management thinking and practice.

Thus, broadly speaking, we can say management is a science with precise universal formulations; which in practice is an art reflecting the cultural variations in societies. Management in India, therefore, must reflect Indian characteristics in its dealings with Indian workers and consumers. And India , it should be remembered, is one of the biggest markets in the world.

Since man is the focus of management attention and his behaviour is influenced by a variety of cultural factors, management science has to be nimble-footed to elicit the best creative talents latent in people. It is in this context that we shall look at management concepts in Vedanta to learn how our ancestors looked at management problems, how they solved them and what were their formulations and insights.

Vedanta is the essence of the Vedas. Vedic ideals, visions and values constitute the world view of an average Indian, governing his self image, life's goals, family and social values. The *Ramayana, Mahabharata, Panchatantra* and various Puranas still exert a great hold on the imagination of the masses and even the middle class, while the great teachings of the *Bhagavad Gita,* as expounded by Adi Sankara, appeal greatly to the Indian elite. Therefore, in understanding Indian tradition and ethos, and thereby the minds of Indian workers and consumers, an understanding of Vedanta becomes imperative.

Another reason for a serious study of ancient lifestyles pertains to the uncertainties, doubts, and confusions in the mind of modern man regarding the direction of industrial progress. Though the engines of industry have created unprecedented wealth, comforts and conveniences, they have also eroded the spiritual basis of human existence, caused unacceptable levels of violence and disruption of the social fabric, with new physical and mental health problems, and ecological imbalances which threaten the very existence of life.

Vedanta unfolds a vision of the individual, of the world, and it discusses the nature of happiness, freedom and work.

"Existence is one integral web, which pulsates as a myriad life forms and matter constellations."

"Truth is one, wise men interpret it variously."

"The world is the dance of Shiva – the Supreme Intelligence."

"God pervades every speck of creation."

"The individual is essentially divine, and vast potentialities are latent in each soul."

When we survey the world of the Upanishads we find some of these startling revelations of Vedanta.

The *Bhagavad Gita*, a consummate Vedanta scripture, unfolds a philosophy of work, taking its cue from the ancient *yajna* practices. It gives valuable lessons on setting goals, motivation, work culture, positive thinking, group dynamics, and organisational behaviour.

The *Ramayana* and *Mahabaharata* are excellent studies of the human mind caught in the ethical and moral dilemmas of the world of business, politics, interpersonal relations, adminstration, the niceties of negotiation and the conduct of war, all within the web of intractable family feuds.

The Puranas are excellent sources of creative imagination and masterly communication techniques to explain difficult ideas and concepts to the masses. Indian management science can learn a lot from these sources in terms of pure theory and in understanding the psyche and thought processes of the Indian economic man.

Analysing the nature of work, the *Bhagavad Gita* says that there are five factors that go into the execution of work. They are the ego, physical and mental faculties, inbuilt values and external forces (*karta, adhistanam, karanam, cheshtah,* and *daivam* respectively). Unless one takes into consideration all these factors and works for their harmonious development, the worker remains a disoriented and disintegrated person, incapable of knowing, developing and executing his *dharma*.

The worker, in his essential nature, is the *atman*, the ever-creative, ever-fresh, eternal source of youthful energy and intelligence. It is only when the worker enjoys his work, regardless of the immediate material rewards, that he can touch this source of inner freshness whereby work becomes supremely enjoyable. In other words, the worker is self-motivated.

In order to make work enjoyable, the worker should be able to identify the work and mode of training that fits his innate nature which is composed of a combination of the three *gunas* or characteristics – *sattva*, (creativity), *rajas* (activity), *tamas* (inertia). A recruitment and training programme which employs this paradigm of thought can understand and communicate better with the Indian mind.

Expanding on work culture, the *Bhagavad Gita* says that people are restless without work and that they are generally group-oriented. They enjoy group activities, chipping in their individual mite. It is this gregariousness of the individual and his zest for work which is to be tapped. The *Gita* uses the words *karma*, *dharma*, *svadharma* and *yajnakarma* to indicate various nuances of work. Karma is individual work, *dharma* is group-oriented work, *svadharma* is group-oriented individual work, and *yajnakarma* means dedicated, egoless, group-oriented individual work. The *Gita* predicts prosperity and peace when society engages in *yajnakarma*. These ideas are embedded in the collective mind of society; we have only to refresh them and reemploy them to communicate a healthy work culture and values.

The *Gita* talks of three ultimate management values – success, prosperity, and justice, leading to liberation and happiness. It should be noted that happiness is a spiritual value and not a function of material conditions. Discipline, moderation, self-abidance, tolerance, and selfless work make one happy. It is this happiness which gives meaning to material affluence, and leads to inner harmony and creative living.

The *Gita* also discusses ultimate freedom (*moksha*) as a fruit of creative dedicated work, regardless of both the ownership and enjoyment of the result. It is the *tamasic*, the mediocre, who want to enjoy the fruits of work. The *rajasic* person enjoys creative work but is attached. The *sattvic* works for the sake of the work without an eye for the possible result, usually the expectation of reward or recognition. It is termed as renouncing the fruits of one's creative work.

The *Gita* lays great emphasis on leaders and its message of renunciation of the fruits of work is addressed exclusively to them, which unfortunately has been turned upside down in an exploitative and authoritarian society, and has been preached to the followers, the downtrodden, to the labourers who only have their physical labour to contribute. No abiding work-culture can be cultivated unless the leaders themselves set standards in living up to the values of renunciation.

These are the ideas which should be considered in an effort to formulate management principles suitable for the genius and temperament of our people. Just as the *Gita* says at the end: "Consider these ideas deeply, give a good thought to them – '*etat vimrsya*' – then come to your own conclusions." I would not advocate religious or cultural fundamentalism or atavism, which will be ruinous for an economy that is trying to find its feet in a highly fluid and competitive world market. We have to be humble, be quite sure about ourselves, including both our strengths and weaknesses. We have enormous intellectual and conceptual powers in which we are second to none in the world. We have deep cultural and spiritual foundations. Let us not repeat the mistakes of others. But at the same time, let us not be afraid of interacting with others, an interaction which will lead us to healthy, wholesome and competitive coexistence. We have to give so that we can take with pride, and in the process, create a new synergy of creative togetherness.

As Gandhiji said, Keep your doors and windows open, so that the fresh breeze from all sides can come in, but don't get swept off your feet by the swift winds that blow across! For this we need a creative insight into our values and traditions. To sell Indian products, we have to sell an Indian vision. Do we have a vision? Perhaps Vedanta can help us in commanding the "vision thing".

1

Meditation

Meditation helps one remain calm and creative in the midst of a busy life. The daily mediator enjoys good health, has an alert mind and a dynamic spirit living in loving harmony with the world around.

Meditation involves sitting in a comfortable posture, creating force fields by either chanting mantras, or practising pranayama to clean up the inner life-stream and controlling the course of thoughts and flow of energy by visulisations, and awakening into the highest form of consciousness, becoming a channel for supreme cosmic intelligence to function in the world.

The meditator is never tired, is ever inspired, though constantly and unremittingly attentive. His awareness is as vast, deep and boundless, ever unperturbed and dynamic, as the borderless blue ocean.

Twenty minutes of meditation in the morning, supplemented by another twenty minutes meditation in the evening will be sufficient to effect desired levels of mutation and elevation in consciousness.

Meditation has to be learnt under the watchful eye of an able guide.

Management Concepts in the Gita

Friends, we are here today in a momentous context. Many changes have taken place in the world. The most important is the death of ideology. Instead of ideologies, man, the individual, is becoming the focus of our attention both in management and in government. Government instead of starting enterprises, is trying only to coordinate activities and individual initiatives. The individual has to take the initiative; it is a kind of capitalistic mode of organising the economy. Earlier, the government used to take the initiative with an ideological goal and motive. And we have seen the failure of that kind of an economic organisation. Modern governments are increasingly abdicating their

Talk at ER & DC, Thiruvanthapuram in February 1994.

economic activities. The latest slogans are: "The less you govern, the better you govern;" "It is not the business of government to do business;" and so on and so forth. I think there is some consensus about these things. So the individual is the focus of management concerns and of governmental activities. The individual has to take the initiative in all economic activities.

Who will make economic choices? What resources are to be pooled into what kind of productive activity? How to distribute the national income, GDP, etc? Since the individual has become the important agent, his choices have become very important. So governments give opportunities to the individual to make his own choices.

The individual is infinitely intelligent. But the paradox is that the more people come together in a crowd, the less intelligence is manifested. The result is usually more discussions, more confusions. All creative achievements were made by the individual – Karl Marx, Einstein, Newton. A group has seldom made a discovery. Individual is the most important factor. If the individual is the important factor, then who is the individual? What is our concept of an individual?

Lately, management science has attempted to understand the individual – whether the individual behind the machine, or the individual who takes decisions. Management gurus take the help of economists to understand what is the nature of an individual.

If you ask a biologist or psychologist, he will say that the individual is no more than a monkey without a tail. Often less than a monkey – just a bundle of suppressions and repression. The physiologist might say that the individual is no more than a couple of electric impulses.

Vedanta has a wholesome and valid concept of the individual. Traditionally, from the Vedantic standpoint, the individual is not just a physical being. The individual has different dimensions. Generally, we think of the individual as a victim of his circumstances. As the circumstances, so is the individual. Therefore, we think of giving all kinds of facilities to enrich the individual. We think in terms of enriching his environment – give him a good spacious office, a wall-to-wall carpeted floor, an office with a view and so on. Generally it is said that if you change the material circumstances of the individual, he can become very creative, very productive, a very good manager. We have tried that method. It didn't work. By changing the environment in which the individual operates, we can of course motivate him a little. But that is not the ultimate solution.

The materialistic conception of the individual is that he is his physical body. Therefore, improve the physical body of the individual – give him exercises everyday – and his performance will improve. That is a Japanese concept. But does he become a better individual?

The individual, others believe, is a product of his physical circumstances. Such experts hold that music can inspire the individual. Therefore piped music in the work place. Or you sit there with music plugged directly to your ears. Can you write an exam that way? Even aeroplane pilots do that. Do we think he can really become a better performer, a better individual, a better worker this way? That also we have tried. It is not the solution. The various methods from the outside to improve the individual have been experimented with and have been found wanting. These methods have not been able to either inspire or motivate the individual. So how do we go about it?

Our concern is to motivate and inspire the Indian worker. How do we upgrade the quality of the Indian work force? How to make the individual work better? What does the Indian tradition have to say about that? What is its concept of the individual?

When a manager looks at a worker, or a boss looks at a subordinate, he generally assumes: "This guy is a lazy person." This attitude sets up an inimical relationship, a sort of antagonistic relationship. We never believe the worker has sincerity. "No, he is a lazy person. I must whip him into activity." The manager begins with a negative opinion, a negative vision of the worker, that he is lazy, that he is insincere, that he is a cheat, unless he proves otherwise by lifelong work. Somewhat like the Indian Penal Code! Until you prove otherwise, you are treated as a criminal. The police will accuse you of committing a crime. To prove otherwise is your responsibility. In other countries it is the government's responsibility to prove that the citizen is a criminal, through various legal and criminal procedures, but till then you are an innocent person.

In the same way, the tendency among managers, top-level executives, the bosses, or the superintendents is to look at their workforce with suspicion: "He is lazy. He is a crook. He is insincere. He has no loyalty to the organisation and he doesn't want to work." The *Bhagavad Gita* (III-5) has a different attitude toward the individual.

Nahi kaschit ksanamapit jatu thishtatyakarmakrt
Karyate hy avashkarma sarvai prakrtijair gunai.

According to the *Gita*, each one is a natural worker, not a lazy person. So when you look at an individual, how should you see him? It is said in the Vedas: "*Mitrasya chakrhusha eksamahe*." Look at him with the eye of friendliness and compassion. The *Bhagavad Gita* says the individual's nature impells him to work. Because he is a packet of energy, he must find expression. The *Bhagavad Gita* holds that the individual needs to work and that he enjoys work.

So let us begin on that positive note. Let us not begin with the thought that the worker is a lazy person. He is naturally a very active person. He wants to work. But we are not able to give him an opportunity, a situation where he can find self-expression. The first step in personality development is to have the right concept about the personality. Let us begin on a positive note, all of us, whether the worker or the manager.

Workers also tend to look upon the manager negatively: "The manager doesn't want to work himself. He lives by exploiting the worker." And there is a philosophy for it also. You see even the management people say: "He is a good manager who works the least. What is management after all, but getting work done through others?" So with the wrong kind of definition and explanation there is no atmosphere of cooperation at all. The worker and the manager should not view each other with suspicion. Remember, "*Mitrasya chakrshusha eksamahe.*" Let us look at each other with the eye of friendliness.

The worker and the manager both inhabit a common enterprise. They have their own different roles to play in productive social activities. They are actually friends, as co-producers, co-workers, working for the same great goals. Each is capable of contributing to this collective activity and each is happy in working. The energy within each is to be used productively. That should be the attitude.

The individual has energy within himself and he wants to express it. He is like a seed – when it is nourished by the earth, the seed finds expression. The seed has the potential within itself. All of us, to begin with, have to understand that we have that energy within ourselves. When you look at another person with this attitude, he gets the message that this person respects me, and that creates an atmosphere of mutual respect. His response will be: "I am a natural worker. By work I am able to discover my potential. By work I am able to discover my identity. It is there within me." The next question is, what is the nature of that individual?

The first statement is we all enjoy work, are natural workers. The second statement is that this individual is a combination of three energies – *sattva, rajas* and *tamas. Sattva* energy is the energy by which we contemplate and create knowledge and value. By *rajas* we restlessly work and move about. And the *tamasic* energy is the dull sleepy aspect of the individual. The indvidual is a combination of these three energies, the *sattvic*, the *rajasic* and the *tamasic*. According to the nature of the work, according to the need of the work, the manager must invoke these various aspects of the individual. If you want the best in an individual in R & D try to invoke the *sattvic* aspect in him. It exists in most individuals. So the top level R & D people have to invoke the *sattva* by getting that kind of training, by eating that kind of food. In developing the *sattva* even food is important. Don't give the R & D man much meat. Let him eat good vegetarian food. Because he has to think. When you eat a lot of meat, your emotions surge forth. And when the emotions surge forth, you tend to become more violent, more aggressive. When you are violent and aggressive you may become a better politician, but not an R & D man. So we have to develop the research people by giving them appropriate food, by giving them the ability to control their emotions, so that their intellect can function. The scriptures stress, "*Shanti,*

shanti, shanti". When the mind is peaceful, the intellect functions, your creativity unfolds. Politicians want revolution and disturbances all over. Their mantra is: "*Kranti, kranti, kranti*" because, on the other hand, when there is disturbance they can sell their ideas.

Research and development is at the cutting edge of economic activity. We are living in a world where ideas are to be created for survival because it is a value-added society, based on value-added products. Most of the economic activities are value-adding activities. You buy a primary product, then you add value to it and create a new product. You have to create new visions for new designs to be created. What are these garment people doing? They buy some fabric, design it and sell it as an exotic garment at an exorbitant price. For that we need *sattvic* people bright in intellect; people like Einstein or C V Raman who were not concerned with ordinary things. An R & D person is single-minded. His energy moves upwards all the time. He is an example of *urdhwaretas,* sublimated energy.

For such an R & D quality a *sattvic* temperament must be developed. If India is to reach a commanding position in the world market, we will have to sharpen our competitive edge and work on those lines. If you want to be competitive, you have to develop an R & D section where visions are created. Everyday you have to create a new idea rather than rehash the same idea day-in and day-out. Then you become a *sanyasi*. A *sanyasi* is a transcendental leader, a person who creates ideas everyday, one who does not repeat the same talk again. That is the kind of leadership quality we require. At least 10 per cent of the workforce must be of really creative people who deal only with ideas and visions, whose *sattva* is in the commanding position in their mind. Such people are to be created. They have to unfold that potential in them.

Another set of people required for economic activity (let us say about 40 per cent of the population), should be *rajasic* in temperament. *Rajas* is another aspect of the personality. *Rajas* is activity, power, organisation. We need organisers also. But don't put the *rajasic* person in *sattvic* work. If you put a *rajasic* person in R & D, he will be thinking of becoming the boss in that department. He is not interested in research. He is not interested in bringing out new ideas. He is interested in name, fame, control and authority.

Consider the case of my compatriot, Mr. M.G.K.Menon, a brilliant scientist. Instead of confining himself to research, he became the Secretary of that particular ministry and, ultimately, a bad politician and a lost physicist. A promising career ended up neither here nor there – *yogabrashta-jatibrashta*. He has become a *jatibrashta* when he might have been another Einstein. Such people lose opportunities to express themselves. They cease to know who they are. They lose their identity. Such people are good organisers, who can create power, and who can use power. The executive and middle level managers are *rajasic* people.

One has to look into oneself and decide to which category one belongs and also into what are the organisational requirements. Do you require *sattvic* people? How many? If an R & D person comes to a manager's post, he will always be lost in dreams, so don't put him there. In such posts you need *rajasic* people. One has to look into oneself and know the *guna* composition of one's personality and accordingly one has to develop skills.

So if you are in R & D, you must concentrate there. You are not after name. You are not after fame. You are not after popularity. You are not after power. Power will run after you. People will come and seek your advice. We need R & D people who just create visions for our community. Any society which does not command a vision cannot survive at all.

And finally we have the *tamasic* people. Everybody, not only a particular section alone, has an element of *tamas* in them, *Tamas* is dullness, lack of interest. You are only interested in *roti-kapda-makan*. If you get your tea daily, if you get a house allowance, then you are happy. You are not motivated by anything else. The only motivation is an opportunity to sleep. However much you may try to motivate them, such people's needs are confined to the physical. In the Maslovain heirarchy of values, they need only the basic creature comforts. Thereafter, the only comfort they want is sleep.

So one has to look into oneself honestly. What is the combination of your personality? How much *sattva*, how much *rajas* and how much *tamas* constitute your individuality. The combination of *sattva*, *rajas* and *tamas* determine your character, your executive ego. Find out your pattern of energy. When we think of unfolding the individual personality, we are trying to develop and train the dominant aspect of your personality.

Everyone is a combination of *sattva*, *rajas* and *tamas*. And when you think of training a *tamasic* person and developing him, you also keep in mind the first two aspects. Even a *sattvic* person will have *rajas* and *tamas* in him. So you have to promote his *sattva* person and try to control his *rajas* and *tamas*. Developing the personality means giving a person the appropriate training and putting him in an appropriate job. Thus one has to discover not only that one is a natural worker, one has to also work according to one's nature, or *dharma*. If you are put in a wrong place, then you become an *adharmi*. So it is essential for the worker to discover his *dharma*. *Dharma* simply means that particular combination of energies. In every organisation there must be training facilities so that the individual can discover his true nature and develop that nature.

Everybody enjoys work, but to enjoy work appropriate training is necessary – in the modern management parlance it is called training and placement. Only then can you invoke the best in you. In the *Gita* two words are used: *karma/dharma* and *svadharma*. Not only must you work, but, if that work is in tune with your nature it becomes your *svadharma*. And

13

when you discover your *svadharma* by a trial-and-error method you enjoy that work. Unfortunately most of the time we are not able to discover our *svadharma*, the work we can happily do. And there are reasons for it. The two most obvious ones are because of your monetary considerations, or because jobs are not available. "I am a University first in physics, but a suitable job is not available. So I applied in a bank. I got a bank clerk's job. And I sit there thinking of physics, quantum theories and all that." And then a customer comes and you are rudely shaken out of your dream and don't understand what he is saying. Nor are you interested in the work. It is because you are doing something for which you are not temperamentally fit. It is a colossal waste of national resources to train a person as a physicist and then place him as a bank clerk. It is a wrong way of planning things. You are killing that individual.

Appropriate training, in tune with one's nature, is essential to discover one's *svadharma*.

When you perform your *svadharma*, you don't do it as an isolated individual. An individual cannot work is isolation. You are always working in a situation as a group. These management experts say: "You want to be an individual, but you want to be a part of a group also." To express your *dharma* through work you have to work as part of a team. When you put several sticks together, they will reinforce each other and each stick becomes stronger than it was as a single stick. So it is with your fingers. Fingers individually have no power. But when they come together as part of a phalanx and when they are supported by the thumb, each finger becomes more powerful than it was before. In the same way, the individual in his effort to express himself, to manifest his latent tendencies and energies, not only has to work according to his nature, but has also to work as part of a team. The *Bhagavad Gita* calls, it *yajnakarma* (B. G. III-35): *Svadharme nidhanam sreyah*.It goes one step further.

It says, in your effort to work according to your nature, even if you die, that is an enjoyable experience – *Svadharme nidhanam sreya paradharmo bhayavaha*.

Since no individual can work independently you have to work as a team. You must know how to get along with people. This is what Sri Rama did. Sri Rama could have straight away gone to Lanka and brought Sita back. He had the power. But he didn't do that. Just to teach all of us, he organised the monkeys, created a powerful army, built a bridge across the water and then went to Lanka, defeated Ravana and brought Sita back. So the teaching is that one has to work as part of a team. This is known as *yajnakarma* or team work.

A word of caution here. *Yajnakarma* or team work is not just team work. *Yajnakarma* is collective effort dedicated to a higher purpose, not a lower purpose. So one has to not only pool the resources of society, or the group, but the organisation must also have an edifying goal. Without an edifying goal, the organisation cannot inspire its workers. Though profit may be the real motive, marketing will couch it in language such as "Consumer is king", or "Consumer satisfaction is the goal". A higher ideal is presented in the same way.

Effective communication

The capacity to get along with people requires communication abilities, which is known as management effectiveness. Think of the top boss. A very efficient man. He comes to the office at 6 o'clock in the morning. and then leaves office only at 8 o'clock in the evening. And in between he doesn't ever take a lunch break. Such a person, who works from morning till evening, is very efficient. He works hard. He is a University first. He has returned from Harvard University. All the data are on his fingertips and he has up-to-date knowledge in his particular field. The pity is that everybody is unhappy with him! He cannot communicate. He can only shout. He always wants to be understood. "You don't understand me," he complains. Watch how often you say that yourself. But have you ever tried to understand than be understood? I can communicate with you when I understand you. Whatever you say is stone-walled by "No." Caught up in his own thoughts, he is not able to understand the other person but keeps chanting the mantra – "You don't understand. Nobody understands me. I have noble intentions. I want to improve the communication system in this city. I am the G.M. I want to improve everything. I want consumer satisfaction." But what about his workforce?

Nobody is happy because he throws tantrums all the time at everybody. He always calls everybody at the wrong hour. He doesn't follow the hierarchy in the organisation. He calls the peon and shouts orders. Everybody is unhappy with him. In effect his efficiency doesn't get translated into efficacy. He is not effective as an organisation man. The problem has to be tackled by developing certain values, communication abilities, a capacity to get along with people, clarity of goals and humility. Humility is a very important value in modern personality development. Unless you are a humble person, you will not be able to unfold your inner potential because you will always be in conflict with somebody or other.

Goals

Now let me recapitulate. First you have to discover your inner nature. Second, you have to work as part of a team. And, thirdly, the collective effort must be offered to a higher altar. Only then does it become a *yajnakarma*. That higher altar has to be defined and every individual has to contribute to that. The organisation must have a clearly defined mission and goal which everybody should know. Even the lowest man in the organisational hierarchy must know the goal clearly and he must feel personally involved. When such an organisational environment is created, you will be able to unfold your inner potential. In this entire philosophy the underlying principle is that the individual is infinitely powerful. In Vedanta we say:

"*Tattvamasi*". You are That. You are infinitely powerful. You have the power within you.

Man is not only a physical dimension. There is an intellectual, mental and spiritual dimension to every individual. How to convince a person that he has got a spiritual dimension? We cannot see it. We are not able to take a photo of that spirit. Each individual must *feel* that there is a spiritual dimension in him. We have techniques for developing the physical dimension – through exercises and good food. And we have the technique of developing the mental dimension through the study of sciences, philosophy, literature, and music, art and culture. We also have techniques for developing the spiritual dimension. Modern management technique tends to disempower the individual whereas Vedanta says: "Give him the power. Make him feel he is great. Make him feel he has it within himself and then invoke it." The individual then knows that he has got a spiritual dimension.

In fact as you work according to your nature, you are unfolding the inner spirit in you and that is true freedom. The freedom of the individual is not just work. The freedom of the individual is discovering his inner dimension, the spiritual dimension, through work and this is happiness also.

What is the ultimate purpose of all human activity? Generally we say happiness, and happiness is conceived as a product of indulgence – the more you consume, the happier you are. That is a Western concept. But from the Vedantic standpoint, it is exactly the opposite. The more you consume, the less happy you are. Happiness is a spiritual value and spiritual function, not a material value.

The Vedantic Ethos in Personality Development

One has to consume less and share more. One has to work without expecting any personal reward. When you are able to work without expecting any personal reward, you are able to freely unfold yourself. That free unfoldment of one's inner potential is true freedom. It is possible only when you work without expectation. A person who works with expectation will have anxieties and tensions, comparisons and agitations and he is not able to unfold his inner potential to the best of his ability. In the *Gita* it is said (XVIII-46):

Svakarmana tam abhyarchya siddhim vindati manava.

Human beings can attain *Siddhi*, the final accomplishment, by worshipping God through work.

Work itself becomes the means of self-expression. In order to transmute work as a means of self expansion one has to understand that one's energy, one's happiness is within oneself.

We have to teach everyone that regardless of the organisational position held, from the top to the lowest man, he has infinite energy. The Upanishads and the *Bhagavad Gita* say: try to organise the energy of each in accord with a collective spirit.

19

Then every individual will be able to discover his inner potential. In the process his personality will grow to whatever dimension it can. Let us not fix a limit to that. Let us not try to bring up everybody to be a hero. Expecting everybody to be a hero is to do violence to the individual. Each individual has a unique nature. The organisation must be able to invoke this uniqueness. That is the genius of an organisation. To bring up all individuals on the same pattern, to the same height, with the same thinking, the same ideas, the same behaviour, the same slogans, is to kill the spirit of the individual. Give the individual an opportunity to take his own decisions. When he is capable of taking his own decisions, he will be able to work according to his nature.

To me it seems that personality development means discovering your personal or true nature, whether it is *sattvic*, *rajasic*, or *tamasic*, and get training accordingly. Then try to work in this world as part of a team for a higher goal. In the process, your entire being becomes intergrated and you are able to develop a highly successful personality. And for this, of course, various techniques are given. A person who wants to be a successful worker must eat good nutritious food, take sufficient exercise, and try to control his negative emotions of violence and anger. At the same time the patience, compassion, love emotions are to be cultivated and edified. And then he must develop intellectual dispassion apart from developing the intellect scientifically and technologically. Dispassion must be developed by cultivating ethical values.

Value Education

Unfortunately the modern man is a confused person because he has been taught no values – there are no points of reference, neither for family life nor for individual life. Certain standards are to be developed for a value-oriented life and you can choose your own values. I don't say that everybody should tell the truth all the time. But how many lies must you tell in a lifetime? Ask yourself, in this particular profession, how many lies should you tell in a lifetime. Only a moderate number! Therefore you have to ration telling lies. Over a period of time, you will have exhausted your quota. Observe some limit. Put some restraint on your emotions. How much should I drink? How many cigarettes can I smoke?

Wisdom lies is putting limits rather than completely abstaining. If you abstain completely, you may become a good man but at the same time be good for nothing. Therefore, I would say you must experiment with everything. You should not be an ignoramous. You must know everything. When you deny something you will know why you are denying it. It is said in the *Bhagavad Gita*, "*mitatva*" (VI-17). *Mitatva* means moderation, setting limits. You should not go beyond the limits set once you have chosen your own value system. Earlier there was a common value because society was less complex, when travel was restricted and technology was less developed. Now there are many more people. People are moving from place to place. Resources are moving. Everything is a constant flux.

Therefore every individual must have his own anchor to find his feet in this flux, his own system of values which is valuable to him personally. He should not live the value of others. That is not wisdom. Values are valuable to him personally. He has to practice them all the time for his own personality development.

So values are to be cultivated. And what is a value? A value is a lifestyle, a state of mind where you are able to live in creative harmony with your surroundings. It avoids inner conflicts and promotes integration within and without, which helps in self-unfoldment. What is most important is self-expression. All other things are secondary to it.

For such a person results are not important thereafter. What is important for him is an opportunity for self-expression. Such an integrated individual, integrated spiritually, intellectually, emotionally and physically, grows to become physically sensitive and his body listens to him. Our problem is that our physical bodies do not listen to us. We know we should not eat *laddoos*. But when we see *laddoos*, we are not able to restrain ourselves. We know smoking is bad. But our physical body won't listen to that. So despite having a value system, you are not able to make your body listen to those values. You become a wretched person in your own eyes. You are not able to integrate yourself. The physical body must obey your orders, your commands.

If we can create such integrated individuals out of our billion people, I am sure India will become one of the greatest countries in the world. That spiritual potentiality must be developed in every individual. Such is the scheme for personality development unfolded in the *Bhagavad Gita.*

You and God

The last sloka of the *Bhagavad Gita* extolls the merit of self-control and the infallible law of self-discipline.

> *Yatra yogesvara Krishno yatra Partho dhanurdhara*
> *Tatra srirvijayobhutir dhruva nitir matir mama.*

Wherever you have this consciousness which is rooted in Divinity, and when you act in this world from that consciousness as a self-giving worker, not for any gross benefit but just to express, just to be yourself, such work brings prosperity, peace and well-being.

By following this practice ultimately you are able to live a happy, prosperous, self- fulfilled life. (B.G. XVIII-78):

Even to discover God, work is the only means. Unless you work without expectation as the means of unfolding yourself, expanding your consciousness, there is no experience of God.

When you are making a product in the factory, let us say stitching shoes or making fabrics, you are trying to discover God in the process. So the question is, can you change your attitude toward work? Can you work as an act of joyous self expression?

Generally we don't understand this truth – that work is a

means of self expression and creating dignity for oneself. Bhagvan says never run away from work (B.G. III-4):

Nahi sanyasna deva siddhim samatigacchati.

We think that to discover God we must run away from work. "After retirement I will go the Himalayas and through Rama-Rama-Rama japa, I will realise Rama." Bhagavan says it is not so. By going to the Himalayas, you are not going to discover God. The God you might discover there can be discovered here also.

Then how can I discover God? Krishna says (B.G. III-9): *Yajnarthat karmanonyatra.* Change your attitude toward work. When you change your attitude toward work and continue to do your work, you are able to unfold your inner potential. That is freedom. That is happiness. It is that happiness all of us are seeking. The usual state is when we are just asking for the gross reward, and a gross result without any regard for satisfaction or happiness. Because a person who just works for an award has no other consideration. That person is going to disintegrate. He will be treated like the silkworm which produces silk around itself. Finally the sericulturist comes, puts the silkworm in boiling hot water and takes the silk cocoon away. Nobody bothers about the worm.

Similarly, if you don't enjoy your work as you are doing it and if you think, "When I get the result I will have enjoyment," you are mistaken. You will be like the silkworm. You keep producing silk, thinking at the end of it you will be happy. In fact you are encasing yourself in a silken prison if you work a 10 or 12-hour day like a robot. Finally you will be finished off in the process. Therefore, while you are doing the work enjoy it. That will be your real reward. The rest are all secondary rewards.

The fundamental question then is can you create a situation where you can enjoy your work? Because that is the only enjoyment, the only happiness, you can get. Yet all of us are pursuing happiness, individual happiness.

Nobody can give you happiness. Even the most philanthropic boss cannot give you happiness. He can give you only money. He can give you various other material incentives. Nor can any government produce it by legislation. No object or goal can give you lasting happiness. When we are thinking of organising a new society, new goals, we have to understand this.

Vedanta very clearly says that happiness is felt *while* you are working. It is not something that will happen after work. Our idea is: "I will work, I will get the result, then I will go to the market, buy a few things, enjoy myself, and I will be happy." I can assure you, you will not be happy. You will get only some comforts. In Russia they tried making people happy by producing material comforts. In America they are trying it. We understand neither of them is really happy. They ignore the real source of happiness.

The philosophy of work must be understood and propagated. Our people are by nature ready for it. It is there in their blood.

First of all, the manager should practice it. Don't preach what you yourself don't practice to your ordinary workers. Work itself should become a source of enjoyment. When the manager is happy all the time, dancing and happy and smiling, then the workers will also follow suit.

Let us understand this philosophy and change our attitude toward work. When you change your attitude all the creativity embedded in the soul will blossom with the enjoyment. Work itself becomes the means of unfolding all those creative energies. Thus we can develop a healthy personality. And when you retire, you will be healthier than when you joined the factory. The usual situation is that when you retire you are finished. You don't know where to go or what to do with yourself. Mind you, longevity may provide 50 years more of life to live in retirement. "Post retirement life" is the latest topic for management seminars. Have you ever thought of that?

A healthy person is one who has lived his life, who has worked with this attitude and in the process has developed a very integrated and centred personality. Thereafter, when he comes out from the factory or the government, after retirement he is happy and contented. He is in perfect health. I would say that he is the most successful individual who comes out healthy and cheerful in the evening of his life.

If you follow this method of enquiry and cultivate an appropriate attitude to work you can lead a happy creative life. If you don't follow it, as Bhagavan said, steeped in your own ignorance, vanity and ideologies, you will have to suffer in life.

Nobody can make you happy. You alone can make yourself happy. Therefore don't work *for* happiness, but work *as* a happy person. Thus develop your inner potential.

Management in Government and Positive Thinking In Creative Management

"Positive Thinking in Creative Management", is a combination of four words. Thinking about managing people (and how to achieve that) is the topic. Before we enter into that subject, it is very important that we take a bird's eye view of what is happening around us. What are we going to think about?

When we look around and survey our economy, along with all that is happening around us in the world, we find a few important trends. The first important trend is that the government is no more at centre-stage. Earlier the government was centre-stage in planning, controlling and executing developmental activities. Ever since the collapse of the Soviet

Talk organised by India Management in Government (IMG) at Thiruvanthapuram in February 1994.

Union, the experience of China and the success of the capitalist economies in creating wealth and employment and distributing wealth in a fairly equitable manner, it is no longer so. We have seen the collapse of the socialist pattern of economic organisation, and the success of the capitalist mode of economic organisation. I will try to share a few ideas with you. You are supposed to be the brains of this state where new values are being churned out and new ideas are being created. So let us set aside all our prejudices and pre-conditioned thinking, and think openly for at least one hour. When we think about it, we find there is, on the one hand, the failure of Socialism, and on the other, the success of Capitalism. We always felt that Capitalism might create wealth, but that it would create it by exploitation of labour, by reducing job opportunities and concentrate wealth in a few hands. As Marx said, a situation will arise of one man owning the entire means of production and people will become unemployed and, finally, there will be a revolution.

The real communist revolution – we were all hoping that the revolution would take place sooner – did not take place, and the totalitarian structures the communist countries created collapsed. In contrast, we find states like Indonesia, Singapore, Malaysia, Taiwan – that were as poor as our country (when we got independence, though we may have been better off in certain areas), have overtaken us. Their GDP has gone up phenomenally. Their per capita income may be ten times more than ours. Generally people enjoy more comforts in those countries.

China too, is thinking on those lines. They have opened their economy. They have done it very stealthily. Twenty years ago they opened their economy. But they preached to everybody, "Don't open your economy. Don't allow foreign capital to enter your country. They will devour you." Now their economy is growing by 14 per cent to 15 per cent, and we are still like a tortoise, moving sometimes at 4 per cent, the celebrated Hindu rate of growth, or sometimes slipping backward.

From these experiences we have to appreciate and accept the superiority of the capitalistic mode of development where entrepreneurs are encouraged. The agents of economic development are not government bureaucrats, or the army, or the police. The agents of progress are the entrepreneurs. It is not the government's business to run business. Their business is to run the government, to play the role of a referee, encourage people, encourage their creativity, allow them freedom, so that every individual has the freedom to make his own choice. That is all the government has to do. The government doesn't have to enter into any of these fields. Its main duty is to see that law and order prevails in the country and that individuals constituting the nation can make choices freely. The government has only to coordinate them.

As I see it, we must take note of this radical change in the thinking of the world economists. Nobody supports the Socialistic pattern of development any more. So we have to think on those lines. How are we going to organise our next step in economic development? The government and the service class have to have an idea about it. In this country the population is divided into two groups – the haves, i.e., the middle class, and the have-nots which constitute 50 per cent or 60 per cent of the population, i.e., the poor people who are below the poverty line. They are about 600 million, which means 60 crores of people.

We, in Kerala, do not know poverty. Though we are poor generally, we don't know the real meaning of poverty. For that we have to go to UP, to Bihar and Rajasthan. This 60 per cent of our population is steeped in poverty. But the Capitalists are heartless people. The middle class is concerned only with its own progress. This 60 per cent of our population which is abjectly poor, has no education, is illiterate, has no access to roads or to medical care, no safe drinking water, no clean clothes. How are we going to uplift them?

I don't think we can entrust this task to the Capitalist or the market forces. The market forces will say, "Get rid of them. We are not concerned with them." Not that Capitalists don't look upon people as a valuable resource, but their main concern is the health of their own capital itself.

I envisage a war in this country between the poor and the middle class, between the values of the middle class and the values of the poor. They are going to clash. Till recently the poor people had at least a philosophy, or even religion which they could live by. The Communist philosophy held that a time will come when everything comes under the control of the state, then everybody will be happy. Religion says, "Don't worry about this world. In the other world you will be happy." I am talking about religion in general, and not about real religion. The religious philosophy and the communist philosophy in a way helped the poor people to live in hope. They could derive some comfort and even inspiration from them.

But now we find that these philosophies have failed and the poor people have no ideology to look up to. There is now only one ideology. That is why the world is ruled by one superpower. And that superpower is crazy. They care for nobody. There is no compassion in their national or their international outlook. They relentlessly, and ruthlessly, pursue their own national interests.

There is a great divide between the Indians, between the poor and the middle class Indians. The middle class Indians are constantly looking to the West. They are linked to the international market. When you go to Delhi or Bombay, it is evident they are not interested in the poor people. They are all interested in how to increase exports, how to earn more foreign exchange, how to send delegates to other countries. Their values, their language, their discussions, everything is conditioned by Western values. So, I think they are delinked from the real India, the India of the poor people.

There is war going on between the poor and the middle

class. What will be the outcome of this war? How are we going to manage this conflict? When I say war, it does not mean a war on Communist lines, with weapons and bullets. It is a political war, fought through the ballot box. How are we going to manage a conflict of interest between the rich and the poor? The role of the bureaucracy, the role of government servants, becomes very important in managing this conflict.

The poor have no capital. They have no ideologies. They have no means of uplifiting themselves and this country. To uplift this country we need entrepreneurs. We need creative people. We need the middle class and their Capitalist ideologies. They are the engines of our economy. We need people who can invest intelligently and make profits, promote this country and sell our products to the world outside. A tiny country like Taiwan, with a population of maybe one crore, if I am correct, has a forex reserve of 100 billion dollars! A hundred billion dollars will be about 300,000 crores of rupees [in 1994 terms]. And our forex reserve is pitiably low. If a country like Taiwan can earn that much and make massive investments in roads, in transport, in education, in human resource development, and health care, naturally the quality of life of their people will be upgraded.

In the modern developmental strategy, foreign reserves become very important. Otherwise there will be no development. And foreign reserves means we have to export. And export means we must have the latest technology. Our workforce should be efficient. We should have certain target areas. This, only the middle class of this country can do. The poor people cannot do it. It stands to reason that there should be a kind of strategic alliance between the poor and the middle class. What kind of strategic alliance? The poor have no financial clout but the middle class knows that the poor can upset their apple cart through the political process and disruptive activities. So, in return for the political peace that the poor people can offer, the middle class offers economic benefits.

I think it will be good if a strategic alliance is forged between the poor and the middle class. This kind of strategy for economic development for this country has to be envisaged as they are doing in Japan and in America. There the bureaucracy, representing people, and the entrepreneur and the business community, representing the middle class, are in close contact. Here we tend to think whoever creates wealth is an enemy of the country. We always think creating wealth is a sin. "How did you make that money?" we ask suspiciously. We presume that making wealth is a devil's job.

I think we have to change that mind-set. Creating wealth, earning foreign exchange and upgrading the standard of living is a divine task. Such a national goal should to be clearly defined. Unfortunately, our politicians are obfuscating. They don't define it clearly. Mr. Narasimha Rao goes to Davos and says, "We have a third, a middle path." What is that middle path, Sir? You have to say clearly whether you want a Capitalist path or not. If you accept the Capitalist path then how do you modulate it? How do you organise it in the Indian context?

The time has come when we have to accept that what we need is a Capitalist mode of development where entrepreneurs – the individual enterprise and individual initiatives – become very important. And this, no government can create. The government can create only a condition, a condition of political peace, a condition where goals are very clear. And once the goal is clear – that of increasing national wealth by exporting more – we have to discuss it across the table with trade unions, government servants, farmers and the unemployed. The task of coordinating and giving everybody a share in the economic growth of the country, and everybody a place in the economic activities – the task of referee, can be done only by the government and the bureaucrats. The government servants will be only the agents – the good agents, the fit agents, for doing that.

This is my perception. It is open for discussion. This is my perception of a strategy for economic development. It is in this scenario that we are going to look at the role of the bureaucracy and government. Of course our bureaucracy is a product of the colonial era when they had absolute power, where power flowed from the heights, from London, and they had only to control the people. They had only to command the people's resources. Whereas after independence, our bureaucracy – when I say bureaucracy, I mean everyone in the entire government machinery – became an agent of economic development. And now a stage has come when government is abdicating that responsibility and wisely so. There is no point in the government taking up the responsibility of daily economic activities. So the third transformation of bureaucracy occurs – from a controlling power to a developmental agency and now just a coordinating centre. It requires great management talents. People have to be persuaded rather than ordered. We have to find the right kind of leaders. That is why we need to think of introducing management values in modern government.

Given this scenario I would like to discuss a few points on positive thinking and human resource development or management in government.

What is positive thinking? To define it briefly, positive thinking means an attitude where you feel, "I can do." This "I can" attitude is positive thinking. But unfortunately our attitude is always negative, "No I can't. It can't be done."

"It can't be done, it is not possible" has become a common word in officialdom. The answer is, "No." I think an expert official is considered to be one who can impede the easy movement of files. The more the file keeps rotating in the corridors of power, the greater is the importance of the officer. Therefore, assuming an obstructive attitude of "It cannot be done," has become the thought pattern wherever you go. I had that experience. When I started an ashram we had to interact with the telephone people, and the electricity people, and the water people. The problems were innumerable – simple problems that they could have solved easily. But they wouldn't because they enjoy exercising power and exercising power means saying "No". Isn't it the same at home? "Mummy, can I go to the movie?" "No." Or, "Mummy, can I read that book?" "No." "Can I talk to that person?" "No." So even if that child talks a few minutes longer over the telephone, Mummy will be standing there. "No." "No" has become an instrument of exercising authority. That is a colonial attitude and it is anti-development.

How do we change? When an entrepreneur comes, instead of looking upon him as a devil – "He is starting a new factory, what is he up to?" – put suspicions aside and look upon him as an angel, as an agent of God. He comes with a new idea to create wealth, to create employment. The bureaucrat or the government official must see that people are encouraged in their modest fields, even opening a pan shop. In whatever field the entrepreneur is engaged, he must be assisted.

That is the right kind of attitude. From today onward, let no bureaucrat say "No" to an applicant. Whoever comes, you must say "Yes". For another ten years let this be the mantra. Always say "Yes" and let us see what is the effect of that. Be determined to say "Yes" all the time. "Can we borrow money from the bank?" "Yes". "Can we fire people, our inefficient employees, who are not working properly?" "Yes." Don't interfere and put obstacles in the way of their work. This way, all the time, a positive attitude is maintained. Unfortunately our national attitude has been negative so far. We have to change otherwise this country cannot progress.

To say "Yes" the goal must be very clear to you. Otherwise you cannot say "Yes" and even if you did there would be no point. It is our duty to have a clear concept, a clear idea of what this nation has to achieve. With that in mind the bureaucrats, the government officials who are going to be the coordinating agency, must always say "Yes".

This is one aspect of positive thought – clarity about the goal and always saying "Yes". This is positive thinking. And creative management? What is creativity? Creativity is tackling a problem in a new way, putting your soul into solving a problem. Don't follow the same old pattern. Our bureaucrats are very lazy people. According to an estimate, the whole of the Government of India can function with one-third of the present strength of employees. Can the country afford the luxury of overstaff? In the government offices people do not come on time. I am talking about North India, I am not talking about Kerala. People don't come on time. They spend a lot of time in gossiping and politicking and discussing promotions. Who got an undeserved promotion? And who is the *chamcha* of whom? This kind of silly talk goes on in the corridors of the Central Government and there is all kinds of manipulation and backbiting. That is because there is no inspiration to work.

There is a story doing the rounds. "In my office there are two types of people. Who are those two types of people? The backward and the forward. Who is backward? One who sleeps in his chair with his back resting on the chair. He is backward. And who is forward? One who sleeps with his head on the table." Then somebody said: "In my office there is a third variety, one who is flatward, who sleeps prostrate on the floor." It is not a joke. It is happening in offices.

I envisage a situation when there will be an exodus from government to the private sector because there is no challenge for a bureaucrat. Policies are often not implemented. There is always interference in their activities. A determined officer, however, can do a lot in this country. K.J. Alphons, for example is doing very good work. He took up a literacy programme in Kerala and was very successful. He is very active now in Delhi. He dreams boldly.

Creativity means doing things in your own way, doing things in a new way rather than in the same old way. And for that the goal should be clear. Creativity means pro-activeness, not reaction. Most of the time we react. A creative person won't react. He will instead invoke his ingenuity, his creativity, and work wholeheartedly. Then alone can he enjoy his work.

There is always a new way of doing things. There are various methods of doing the same thing. Therefore we must try to invoke that creativity from within ourself by trying to do things using different methods and ways. Everyone can, if they try.

One must take it up as a challenge. This development work, or economic progress, is going to be very chaotic because we have no model now. The Chinese have given us certain leads in how the government can become an agent in encouraging entrepreneurs but we must evolve our own way of doing things. The bureaucrats or government officials should try to invoke that inner creativity to try to do things newly. Always say, "Yes, I can do that! We will do that. We can do that together." This is the kind of attitude to be created. Creativity in doing things, taking up the challenge and offering solutions in new ways.

And finally management. Why management? Management is crucial, because people have become very important. The central concern of modern management now is people whereas earlier it was machines, money or resources. The individual is the greatest resource. Earlier we thought the individual is only a drag on everything, merely another mouth to be fed. Then we realised that not only has he a mouth to be fed, but he also has two hands to work. And he has a brain to think. He can create ideas. So the individual as a producer, or as a worker and consumer has become the centre of management concern. How are we to inspire the individual as a producer or as a worker and as a consumer?

If the main problem is how to inspire the individual what are the methods of inspiring a person? It is said that the individual can be inspired by giving him a new vision, a new idea about himself. Generally we look upon the individual as a limited, lazy, miserable person. This is especially so in the case of a superior who tends to look down upon subordinates. "He won't work," is the attitude. When an efficient officer talks to subordinates, his attitude should really be: "I am not able to inspire him, not that he is lazy or corrupt. I am not able to touch a deeper level in him." When there is interaction between the superior and the subordinate, the officer and his assistants, the attitude of the officer should be that all individuals enjoy work.

That is what the *Bhagavad Gita* says (III-5): "*Nahi kascit kahanmapi jatu tishtyakarmarkrt.*" People enjoy work. Work gives them dignity. Work gives them self-worth. The old attitude – "Nobody wants to work," doesn't hold good. The fact is everybody wants to work, but we don't know how to motivate them, how to inspire them. When we look at an individual in our office, at our subordinates or at our colleagues, the attitude should be that this individual has infinite potential. That is the central theme of Indian philosophy.

"*Amrtasya putra srunvantu*" – Listen O children of immortality. Whatever he may be, a Brahmin or a low class servant in your office, each individual is infinitely powerful and potent. Can we look at an individual with this attitude? Can we look at him with the conviction that the man in front of me can be inspired infinitely, that he can be made to do work provided I can inspire him!

When we study our Puranas, the instances of Hanuman and Sri Rama are classic examples of inspired work. Sri Rama had to go to the forest, there Sita was abducted by Ravana. Now Rama had to retrieve Sita. He could have asked for help from Ayodhya: "Please send an army." Rama didn't do that. He looked for readily available resources. He had a few monkeys as assistants. Usually monkeys are very restless animals jumping up and down on the trees. What could Rama do with these kind of monkeys? He had to fight with the mighty Ravana who had *rakshasas* in his army – very powerful people who could fight at night. They had night vision. And there was Indrajit, a great warrior, the conqueror of Indra. Rama had to contend with all this. But Rama did not get disappointed or frustrated. He organised a mighty army with the help of these monkeys. Not only did he organise an army, he also built a bridge from this subcontinent to the island. Nor, when he came to the seashore, did Rama say, "Now what will I do? There is this mighty ocean between me and Lanka. What will I do now?" He did not sit about discouraged. He found a way of building the bridge and he went across. Rama did not complain about his workforce. There is a Tamil saying: "*Vallabanu pullum ayudhuam.*" For the dexterous, even a blade of glass serves as a mighty weapon. But if an individual is not efficient, even an intercontinental ballistic missile will not do.

Therefore, power lies not with the machine, but with the man behind the machine and the inspiration that he is capable of. He has to draw inspiration from within himself and inspire others, as a leader alone can do just as Rama inspired the monkeys and forged a mighty fighting machine out of them, fought Ravana, and retrieved Sita and his honour. Let us now consider Hanuman. Hanuman was an unemployed monkey because he was the minister of an unemployed king. The king had no kingdom; he had only a barren rock to lord over and nothing to administer. So Hanuman, though he was infinitely powerful – he was "*Nava-vyakarna-pandita*", a great scholar, and also "*Vakchaturyam*", a great communicator and a great personality – nothing shone forth because nothing inspired him. He had nothing to do. He was simply marking time. One day Hanuman saw Rama. And the moment Hanuman saw Rama, everything fell into place. And Hanuman became one of the mighty heroes that our country has produced.

Hanuman never said "No" to anything. In the battlefield, people were lying unconscious. The doctor said, "I need a special medicinal herb from the Himalayas." Hanuman did not say, "I don't know whether a flight is available. Or, will I be able to get there in time? He didn't complain, 'I have a backache, haven't I done enough? Why only me?' He didn't say, 'Maybe tomorrow morning'. Or make excuses, 'My wife is sick'." He said, "All right, Hey! Ram," and took off. When he reached the Himalayas, unfortunately he realised that he had forgotten the slip of paper on which the medicine's name was written. He didn't say that he would go back. Hanuman simply lifted the whole mountain, and flew back. Look at the sincerity of that worker! Rama and Lakshmana were saved by his effort.

This is the kind of spirit that manifests itself when we inspire a person. Then there is nothing impossible for that person. Our challenge is to first define our goal very clearly. Without doubt there will be conflicts. But we have to give everybody a place. The government needs to play a greater role in defining our national goals, in commanding a national vision for the future and then inspiring people.

All those activities are beyond the capability of our politicians. You, the thinkers, and institutions such as yours, have to take the lead. You have to communicate with people, the trade union leaders, the poor people, the farmers, and various sections of the society. You have to go to universities and create this national consensus about economic activities or the mode of development that we need. Your institute can do a lot. And the government can do a lot. Government servants – I am not talking about politicians – can do a lot. And I want you to rise to that expectation. May God bless you in that effort.

Spiritual Dimensions in Modern Management

Today's theme is a very interesting, very challenging theme "Spirituality and Management". Somebody said that there are two bogus sciences – one is management and the other is macro-economics. I should add one more. Spirituality is another phoney science if you don't understand what it is all about. Yet it is a very interesting study and the more we go into that, the more we feel its importance. This attempt to adapt spirituality to management practices is ongoing. Our country has a rich spiritual tradition in the Upanishads, the *Gita*, Puranas, *Ramayana*, *Mahabharata*, *Panchatantra*, Kautilyasastra, Panini Bhashya and Manusmriti. We have a rich repertoire of spiritual

Talk to National Institute of Personal Management (Thiruvanthapuram chapter) in March 1994.

tools by which we can enhance human efficiencies, efficaciously and innovatively. We can enhance our capacity to get along with people. These are the kind of values our spiritual literature has to offer.

I believe that spirituality can be effectively integrated into modern management science – science or art or whatever you call it. We will come later to the question: How is it possible?

Our country is opening up and we find invasions from all sides – from the sky and from the sea, intellectual and ideological, multinationals and new products are coming and we are responding with trepidation. We don't know what to do. Some of us say close the borders, throw away the Dunkel Draft, don't sign the GATT Agreement. They will flood us and our values will be eroded. On one hand our economy is opening up and we have to face great challenges and, on the other hand, we are not sure about ourselves. Neither is our track record that creative, nor as individuals are we confident of facing this challenge. So the nation as a whole, and every individual who is a part of this nation, is looking for values, visions and techniques by which he can become an effective competitor in the world market. Unless you sell India, you cannot sell an Indian product. So how do we sell ourselves?

To sell ourselves, we must have self-confidence. We must have a certain pride in our tradition, our culture and our way of looking at the world and experiencing life. And for that an understanding of our culture is necessary. And fortunately modern management is now talking about the individual. The individual as a worker and as a consumer has become the focus of our management concerns.

The Spiritual Dimension

So what exactly is the individual? Has spirituality something to say about that? And when we say spirituality, we should definite it. What exactly is spirituality? What kind of spirit is that? Not the kind that some may take every evening. What exactly is the spirit we are talking about? We talk of matter, mind, spirit, consciousness, intelligence, conscious, unconscious, collective unconscious, creativity, spontaneity and so on and so forth – but what exactly is the significance of those words?

Very simply we can say that spirituality or spirit, is something which is very intangible. You cannot pinpoint it. You cannot put it in a bottle and say: "Please have a look at it and pass it on." A laboratory experiment is not possible with spirituality. The spirit is something intangible, something invisible.

In fact one definition of the spirit is that which cannot be seen, that which cannot be thought of. Anything which you see, which you can think of, which you can handle, which you can manipulate, measure and control is not spirit. In Vedanta we call this *maya*, that which can be measured, that which has a dimension, which has existence, an externality which you can see and touch and handle and control. The spirit, however,

49

is something which is invisible, which cannot be contacted, which cannot be measured.

Somebody from a leading management institute said to me that he had devised a mathematical formula for measuring consciousness. But the first definition of consciousness is that which cannot be measured. The moment you try to measure it you have killed it. Then you think of manipulating it, of improving it, of shaping it according to your petty little notion about things because you cannot stand unpredictability. You cannot stand something you cannot know. The very definition of the spirit is that which cannot be measured, which cannot be handled, which cannot be seen. But you can feel its presence. As Ramakrishna said when Vivekananda asked, "Have you seen God?" "Yes, my dear boy, I see God perhaps with much more clarity, than I see you." That kind of an expression – though it cannot be measured, though it cannot be quantified and still it is there, may sound paradoxical. To know the spirit you need a certain sensitivity. And unless that sensitivity is developed, you will not be able to understand what it is. As someone said this morning: "There was some higher power coming upon me, descending upon me. When I was in a crisis, I did not know what to do, like Panchali, and I collapsed. In the process I found myself collapsing at the feet of the Lord, and somebody was lifting me up." That is a function of a certain sensitivity. I would not call it faith since you are not sure about it. If you had that kind of a faith it might not have happened, because

God knows anyway when you have faith.

So the spirit is something which cannot be measured, but still its existence can be felt in a different way. At unexpected moments, when you feel everything is at sixes and sevens and the world is a mess around you and you feel you cannot go any further ahead, suddenly you experience a shower from beyond. Your whole life gains a new spring. And you start seeing flowers blooming everywhere and there is a new message, a new energy welling up from within you.

That is the dimension of the spirit. You may not be able to quantify it. You may not be able to convince somebody of its existence unless that somebody is ready to learn. If you look at it with a suspicious eye you will not see it. As Bhagavan says in the *Gita* (IV-40): "*Samsayatma vinasyati.*" If you keep on doubting it you miss it. But if you are alert and if you are intelligent about it, some time or the other you will be blessed by it.

The spirit is an intangible value and expresses itself as self-confidence, love, compassion, understanding, faith, a feeling and care for the other and the belief, or at least a glimpse, into your own inner potential. Even if the whole world said you are useless you know you are not useless, but only being used less. You *know* that. That is the kind of an inner sensitivity, even when the whole world is against you, or because they have got their own interests whereas you are your own best well-wisher. So when you look at yourself from that standpoint, you find new doors opening, new dimensions appearing, new suns rising in your life, And you find a vast area of consciousness, a continent of consciousness, opening up for you. That is what I mean by spirituality. When you work on the spirit in you, new energies arise in you. We think of spirituality when we have exhausted all other sources of energy. For examples, we have developed our muscles, we have developed our intellect, we have tried to manipulate our emotions by various methods. That is what the modern psychologists are doing. They try to adjust our ego with minimum pain to the social needs. We have engineered our emotions. There is engineering of behaviour and emotions in the universities and institutions. We have done all this. And still, at the end of it, we find a tortured, miserable and persecuted individual. An individual without self-expression, without self-knowledge.

It is this situation which thwarts the unfolding of that inner potential. Without it we find ourselves lacking in energy, and are utterly tired and confused. Nobody is able to motivate us. That is what happens to Arjuna in the battlefield. Arjuna is a highly qualified person. In fact he has got a new degree from Shiva, a Ph.D. degree, if I am permitted to use this expression, and a new weapon in his armoury – straight from Lord Shiva, the Pasupata. So he is highly qualified. He has great war strategies. He has won various battles. He has fought great warriors and won. He went to heaven and come back.

He was not lacking in anything. We can see Arjuna as highly qualified, technically competent and the whole world recognises his abilities. In fact a few corporations were vying for his sevices: "Can you come and join us?" He is not an unwanted, unemployed person. He is a highly qualified and reputed person. He has proved his worth in various battles. And it is that Arjuna, who at the critical moment of his life collapses in the battlefield of Kurukshetra and says: "Oh Lord, I have no energy, I am tired. I am running away from the battlefield."

Motivation

The whole of the *Gita* is a motivational scripture. "Arjuna you have to fight this battle," says Bhagavan who then tries to motivate Arjuna in various ways. The most important goal of management is to motivate people. How to motivate them to do their alloted work, and to play their respective roles?

Bhagavan tries to motivate Arjuna by various methods. The first method was to call Arjuna names. It is a tendency we all have. Haven't you ever said, "You are a useless person. You are a stupid peson, live up to your manliness." It is also what Bhagavan said (B. G., Chapter II-2, 3):

Anaryajusta masvargyam akirtikarama Arjuna,
Kutastva kasmalamidam vishame samupastitam.

Arjuna what is happening to you? You are an Aryan. You

belong to a great race. You are highly qualified. You are the disciple of Drona, one of the greatest masters. You have passed from Drona's institute, in the same way you pass from the Ahmedabad Management Institute. You too are a first-class first rank student of that institute. After all this, now you want to turn back! Bhagavan says, "*Kutastva kasmalamidam vishame samupastitam akirtikaram Arjuna*." What do you really lack? Haven't you got all the energies?

Bhagavan also tries to invoke Arjuna's valour, his sense of pride, his sense of ego, his sense of belonging to a certain family and a certain country, to a certain tradition. Bhagavan was trying to reach that and bring him back to normality. But Arjuna did not respond to those exhortations. Arjuna said: "This I have heard a lot. People praising me, telling me that I am the best in the country, therefore I must work hard. But I am not motivated by that. You may remind me of my family tradition, my degrees and the honours and awards I have received. I have seen through all that. I am not at all inspired."

Then Bhagavan tried another tack, a bit of emotional blackmail. He said, "Arjuna this will cause you lasting ill-fame. If you don't fight this battle, what will the others say about you? (Don't you ask what the other company people will think? What the other man will think? What the neighbours will think? What your own children will think?) To stress the result of the lasting ill-fame we can imagine him continuing: "There will be illustrated comics about you, the shameless manner you ran away from the battlefield. All the newspapers will write in bold letters that Arjuna ran away from the battlefield and then it will be a very shameful experience for you. Bhagavan was merciless and said, (B. G., II-34) *Maranadadirichyate.* – "It is worse than death, Arjuna! You are self-destructive. What you are doing is suicidal." Arjuna looked up for sometime but again he collapsed and said: "This does not interest me. I don't care what others say about me. I have gone through that also. I am not a little child now to look to the outside world for praise and recognition. I can stand on my own." Arjuna maintains: "I am not interested, I am not inspired by that."

That graded method of motivating also fails. Then Bhagavan says: "Arjuna look at your own duty – this is your duty – this is the call of duty. The nation needs you, the country needs you. Your organisation needs you. Therefore, Arjuna you have got an opportunity to respond to the call of the nation." Remember Bhagavan was trying to inspire Arjuna by mentioning national glory and appealing to his patriotism. At the time of Gandhi let us recall Bhagat Singh, who walked with a smile to the gallows. But Arjuna says: "I am an international man. I am not interested in patriotism. These are all the old world values. Now we live in a global village where people interact globally. I have gone beyond national boundaries. And you cannot inspire me by that." Arjuna insists, "I am not going to fight this battle."

These are the techniques we employ – by appealing to our

national pride, by appealing to our family pride, by appealing to our various glories, the prospect of fame and recognition we will command in society. The boss is trying to inspire you. You are not inspired. And then the last method is to give you a *Sramavira* award. Having got it for another year, you may work. The following year somebody else gets that award. Therefore you are again demotivated.

How do we motivate an individual?

Finally Bhagavan realises that these external props – these external crutches – will not work. What will work, is to give Arjuna a new self-identity, a new self-image. Make him see who he is, what are his powers, what is his infinite inner worth. Bhagavan gives Arjuna a new sense of himself, that he is not just Arjuna. He is not just his father's son. He is not just a citizen of this country. He is something more. Bhagavan gives him a new idea about himself. That is why in the second chapter of the *Gita*, we find the Lord saying (B. G., II-11): "*Panditah nanusochanti.*" *Pandita* means an enlightened person. Who is an enlightened person? One who has come to grips with himself, a man who has understood who he really is. A person who has understood his true nature is an enlightened person. And what is his true nature? According to the *Bhagavad Gita*, you are Infinite. You are happiness. Your nature is happiness. You don't have to *do* anything to be a happy person.

Happiness is your true nature

Friends, the fundamental defect in all our undertakings is that we are always busy *doing* something to be happy. And the more we try to be happy, the more unhappy we become. Is it not so? All the time we are trying to be happy, by shifting from one chair to another chair, from one place to another place, from one factory to another factory, from one organisation to another organisation. We keep on changing. We even change our names. Become a *sanyasi* and gain a new name – Sadananda becomes popular, and he goes to the West. And there people cannot pronounce his name properly. They always call him Sad-ananda. And then he comes back as Sad-ananda! We change everything in an effort to be a happy person. What a pity! We don't realise that happiness is our nature. To be a happy person we don't have to do anything. We have just to relax, loosen up, and be natural. So when you relax and are natural, then you are a happy person. There is really no gap or distance of space between you and happiness.

When we say 'spirit,' in Vedanta, it means this happiness which is your natural state. There is no other spirit that Vedanta talks of. There is no other god that Vedanta talks of. In no uncertain terms Vedanta says that you are the source of happiness. And in discovering that I am the source of all happiness, I become spiritual. I don't have to depend upon any external situation. My situation has no bearing on my happiness. I am happy inspite of the situation. A person who has come upon that self-discovery, that rootedness, that self-identity, can be called an enlightened person. People maintain that gaining enlightenment is very difficult. "I have to sit in a particular contorted posture to be an enlightened person. I have to stare at the tip of my nose. Unfortunately my nose is a little flat therefore I cannot look at it. So how can I mediate?" Bhagavan says you don't have to do anything to be a happy person. You don't have to place yourself in a particular posture to be happy. You don't have to change your name or lifestyle to be happy.

The fact is happiness is your natural state. Nor do you have to have any training for happiness. The best expression of happiness is a smile. That is the only exercise you have to do, learn to smile. Somebody asked how you define smile. Do I have to define something which is very natural to you? There is a craze for definitions. "How do you define smile? Can you show me a chart of a smile? What happens to the metabolic activity when I smile?" These questions are not important for us. We are unnecessarily messing up our life by charts and words and definitions. A smile is very natural to you. Smile, and your spirits soar. Pull a long face, and the spirit goes down under. Is it a great effort to smile? Is there any school for smiling? There is no school necessary for smiling. That is what you come into this world with. You have forgotten the art of smiling because of your stupid ways of living. You have lost that intelligence.

So who is an intelligent person? An intelligent person is one who is naturally happy, who can face a problem with a smiling face. And when you can face a problem with a smiling face, we guarantee that the solution will emerge from within yourself. You don't have to look outside for solutions. In fact, according to spirituality, all those great values that you seek in life like health, intelligence, energy – all those will spring from within yourself.

Unfortunately, for intelligence, we tend to read a lot of books and we tend to become an intellectual. An intellectual is one who has an opinion about everything. "What is your opinion about Ayodhya? What is your opinion about modern management? What is your opinion about this and that?" One who is ready with an opinion, one who is burdened with conclusions, is one who has a blocked mind. He is a dead person. He cannot look at a problem freshly, spiritually, through his own eyes. He looks at the problem through borrowed eyes. A spiritual person is one who is naturally comfortable with himself, who can look at a problem with a smiling a face. This is what we mean by saying leave everything to God. What does that mean? It means you have faith in yourself. You have that spontaneity. You don't have to approach problems with a readymade set of solutions.

Unleashing Creativity

When you approach a problem with a fresh, open mind,

solutions spring up from yourself – fresh blossoms will bloom from inside yourself. Don't be satisfied with plastic blossoms. When you go with a set of solutions borrowed from here and there, you are going to miss the joy of solving a problem. You will get only plastic flowers. These do not have any fragrance though they may last long. For every problem, you will have a set of everlasting solutions or plastic flowers. But no butterfly will come to them. No bee will come around them. They have no fragrance and honey. They have no life.

In the same way, when we look at a problem freshly, spiritually from our own standpoint, then solutions come. That is why Bhagavan says, "*Panditah nanusochanti.*" He invites challenges. He loves uncertainties. Because uncertainties inspire him. In a situation where everything is defined, he feels sleepy. Some of you sleep even during such lectures because everything is predictable. The first opening statement is predictable. The end statement its predictable. In between it is always predictable. Therefore you feel sleepy. There is no challenge at all. A person who wants to discover the divinity within himself, that energy within himself, to lead a healthy, intelligent and creative life, must always live in uncertainty. Therefore we must accept the present situation of economic uncertainty. It is a challenge for us. Let all our borders be opened. Let everybody come into our country. Let us interact with them. Why are we afraid? Are we not infinitely creative?

We have been great creators and innovators in ancient times.

Why don't we recapture the same spirit? It is possible. Hence Bhagavan says an enlightened person, an intelligent person, is one who has rootedness in the spirit. And the spirit manifests itself when you simply smile. New theories, new visions, new ideas will emanate from you. We are not such a shallow civilisation; we are not a shallow set of people. When you talk with a smile to your customer, your subordinate, your children, your own wife, you will get cooperation. Ask your wife with a smile, "Get me a cup of tea." She will bring it. If you say with a frown, "Get me a hot cup of tea," she will probably bring you a cold cup of coffee. And she will say, "I was busy, don't you know? If you want one so much, go and make it. Make one for me also." If you don't talk with a smiling face, nobody is going to listen to you, because you are blocking their intelligence. When you block your intelligence in the process you are blocking everybody's intelligence and there is a complete blockage of intelligence and then you find people get bored, yawn and have no energy to exercise at all. So in our search for energy we are not looking outward, we turn inward. "*Avrtha chakshuh*," it is said (*Katha* II-1-1).

Generally people are extroverted, they look outward – "*Paranchikani vyatrnat svayambhuh*". That is the way to destroy yourself. But when you look inward, you will touch a great source of energy. That was the secret of the energy of Mahatma Gandhi, Bhagat Singh, and Jesus Christ. What gave strength to Jesus Christ? He was hanging from the cross on three nails and blood was dripping and Christ said: "Oh Lord forgive them." What is the source of that statement? It is not out of a calculating, manipulative mind that such statements arise. It is from a still, deep, fresh, untapped source of spiritual energy. That was the source which made Christ say, "Oh Lord forgive them." Gandhi said the same thing. Lord Rama said the same thing. When Rama was asked to go to the forest, he went with a smiling face.

The first priniciple in spirituality is that though it is an invisible value, it is there for you to tap. You can become sensitive to it, you can invoke that energy in your daily life, in your ups and downs, and in your conflictual situations. It is not available only in the seat of meditation. It can be realised, and experienced when you come out into the work-a-day-life-world, in the market place, in the dust and din of daily living. In fact when you interact with the world, in the turbulence of everyday challenges, you will be able to continuously experience that energy as a continuous creativity streaming forth. It is not a spasmodic experience. It is continuous. Ramana Maharishi says (*Upadesasaram*, -7), "*Ajyadharya stotasasmam.*" Even as you pour *ajya* or ghee (clarified butter) from one vessel to another, it flows without any break. In the same way, your creativity can be unbroken and effortless, like the flow of a river. The river never stops to say, "I am tired of flowing, please give me a helping hand." The river is continuously flowing. The more it flows, the more it gathers energy, momentum and enthusiasm because it is going to meet its Lord the mighty ocean.

In same way, an efficient person – a person who is effective in his life – is one who has touched that source of energy. And friends, that source of energy is freely available. But, unfortunately, we are ignorant about it. What a tremendous loss of national resources, of individual potential. We live like blind people not knowing that there is a gold mine hidden where we sleep. Instead we take a begging bowl and go begging for an award, for recognition, for a promotion, for a position. "Give me some inspiration, some enthusiasm. I am not able to work without that, otherwise I feel sleepy and demotivated." This kind of a slavish and beggarly attitude is not experienced by a realised person.

A realised person is one who looks into himself for inspiration. He doesn't say that this is possible only for managers. It is possible for everybody if you touch that source. When a manager puts his arm around his worker and smiles and asks him how he is, that is sufficient motivation for him. He will put in his maximum because he also wants to work. The *Bhagavad Gita* says, "*Nahi kaschit khsanmaapi jatutishtatyakarmakrt.*" To sit idle is bondage, is a burden. Nobody wants to sit idle. The greatest punishment is solitary confinement, or not being allowed to do anything.

Since one must work, because individuals are so constituted, what should be the attitude with which one undertakes work?

Generally, work causes anxiety regarding the results. There is no guarantee that the worker will get the expected result, and that uncertainty produces tension. Bhagavan says that work must be undertaken with the karmayoga attitude or *yajna* spirit, so that tension and anxiety can be avoided. With that attitude work is transformed into a means of self expression – a continuous experience of inner bliss.

What is meant by the *yajna* spirit? Does it point to a work culture? And can it become the basis for an emerging Indian work culture?

The Yajna Spirit

The first step in *yajna* is pooling your resources – it has to be team work, a cooperative effort. The pooled resources must be offered then at a higher altar as in *yajna*. If this offering does not take place, it is not a *yajna*; it is only a collective activity. In the Communist countries they tried it. They came up to the pooling of the resources, but there was no offering at a higher altar. When you offer resources at a higher altar, your collective energy gains a new strength. When you pool your energy, every individual in the group gains new strength through mutual reinforcement. A synergy is created. And this synergy, when offered at the altar of a higher principle, activates the cosmic benediction which flows through that offered energy, and through that dedicated activity unmatched results are generated. There is collective success. Whatever you do, becomes successful.

These are the things you have to experiment with. Whenever you work for a higher ideal, there is greater enthusiasm, greater energy manifestation. And there is greater joy also. The lesser the ideal you work for, the lesser the enthusiasm, lesser energy and there is no joy at all. So we do have a work culture in the *yajna*.

In the Vedas there are descriptions of how to collect resources, and how to propitiate various Gods. If you want rain, propitiate Indra! If you want wealth, propitiate Lakshmi. And who are these Gods? These Gods are none other the cosmic intelligence and its various manifestations in life.

When we work together and offer work a higher altar, we become beneficiaries. There is benediction flowing from the higher altar and the cosmic intelligence blesses. All undertakings that you initiate become successful.

So friends, we do have a work culture. We have beautiful terminologies for it. Concepts like *karma*, *dharma*, *yajna*, *yajnakarma*, *nivedyam*, *prasada*, etc., are beautiful concepts. If you tell your worker, "Your work is a *nivedyam*," he will understand it. He instantaneously understands what *nivedyam* is. He knows *nivedyam* is that which is offered at a higher altar. He also knows that if work is *nivedyam* at a higher altar, what comes of it becomes *prasada*. And if it is *prasada*, he won't react to it. He will work free from tension.

2

Management

Management is another field of study which Swamiji strongly feels will be enriched by critical and creative interaction with visions and values born of spiritual insights and meditation.

Inspiring people at the work place and managing the human mind for creating wealth within acceptable psychological, social and ecological cost, is the major challenge for modern management. In this context human resource development by self-motivation and self-actualisation, through meditation and expansion of consciousness by dedicated work becomes of significant value. And defining happiness, in the pursuit of which human societies are organised in productive relationships, as essentially a spiritual value gives the science of management a spiritual foundation and moral orientation.

Management Lessons from Patanjali's Yoga Sutras

In preparing our people to face the challenges of the 21st century, the Management Association of Ahmedabad (AMA) has been in the forefront of promoting management culture. The world is increasingly becoming a single space and the forces of competition require us to prepare ourselves, as individuals, as organisations, and as the country as a whole, by focusing on our strengths. The situation is so grave, and the urgency so palpable, that we can no longer afford to wait thinking that time will solve all problems.

As you know the character, goal, the ambition and the sense of fulfilment of a society is determined by its culture which it has nourished over a period of time. A society which is uprooted from its culture, whatever the reasons, will not be able to face the challenges confidently. This is the background – that we are going back to our own culture to gain an understanding of the way in which our forefathers faced problems and sought solutions. It is very important that we find our roots, otherwise we may lose our own self, our character, our individuality. Loss of that will deny us power to create synergies for the greater welfare of our people and the world. I repeat, we must gain rootedness in our culture.

Fortunately, our culture is so great that it has infinite creativity and manifold survival techniques. We carry those survival genes in us. We have only to develop them, and modify them, to help us face the modern challenges. It is important that we not only look forward into the future, but also look backward and inward and strike deep roots in our spiritual culture so that we can spread our civilisational branches heavenward. It is in search of this synergy, in search of our ancient roots, that these series of lectures are conceived. The understanding of our past is wisdom, a collective intelligence of how we look at the problems of life. Hence it is appropriate that management institutes take up this mission of introducing our culture to management-learning because no management decision is taken independent of our cultural context.

There was a time when management pundits thought that management decisions were secular, objective in nature and had no subjective cultural component. But now they realise that since management is basically about motivating people, no economic decision can be taken without reference to the cultural context. For successful management practices one has to know the ethos and the essence of Indian culture.

Recently, in a Round Table conference, we were trying to discover the essence of Indian management. In USA they identify the "hire and fire" policy as the essence of American management. In Japan it is "life long security". But what is the essence of Indian mangement? All the participants, leaders and academicians were breaking their learned heads on this topic: How to define Indian management distinct from management in other countries? We could not define Indian management, but we arrived at a practical definition: Indian management is that which works in India. Then we went into another issue – "What is the essence of Indian culture?" The consensus was: "Respect for age" and "Respect for the dissimilar". Respect here means an appreciation of the uniqueness of the individual, and the acknowledgement of the spark of divinity in him. In fact divinity means uniqueness. When I look at another individual with that eye, respect becomes natural.

In India the foundation for a new management ethic, or a management scripture if I may say so, should be "mutual respect". In our teaching institutions, which are supposed to create and disseminate knowledge, the value for "respect" is missing. Nor is there respect for elders in the family, or respect for leaders in society. The result is that our leaders have become opportunists and are not willing to think strategically and plan for the long-term future.

Our culture is based on respect for the other. This may not conform to whatever we have learnt from management institutions of the West, but as long as it works, as long as the goods are delivered, it is okay. Based on these two ideas, that "it should work in India," and should flow from "mutual respect", various institutions are engaged in putting together a "manual of Indian management".

Indian culture, as you know, is based on the Vedas. Vedas means knowledge; they unfold a vision about the world which is holistic, integral and spiritual. Vedas envision the world as one organism, whereas Western science looks upon the world as a machine which can be dismantled and assembled again. That, however, is not possible with human beings. There is something in the individual which makes him alive as a person, something indivisible and holistic. If the world is more like an organism and not like a machine, and every individual is part of the world, tinkering with the world will create difficulties.

While we have achieved great progress in science and technology, productivity and mass production of goods and services, at the same time we find ecological problems and erosion of family and community values. On one side we have progress but we also have the invisible costs of progress. How are we going to tackle this problem?

The West does not have this holistic view. They concentrate on the particular and miss the totality. The holistic vision of the Vedas unfolds an answer to the modern management dilemma of development versus environment.

Vedas say that both are important. We need development, and we need environmental health. How do we strike the balance?

Another problem of modern management is the ethical issue – how far can we integrate ethics and human values into management practices? Is profit the sole motive of management, or should humanistic values be factored into profitability? The Vedas dealt with and answered these questions long ago.

Health is another problem. Modern executives may be great achievers, but at the age of 40-45 years, they fail in health. The ecological problem and the health problem together constitute the greatest challenge to modern management which is grappling with the problem of production and development. All these need to be looked at from the perspective of a given culture. We have our own culture and tradition and it is in this context that we are going to discuss Patanjali.

Who was Patanjali, and what was his contribution? Patanjali is believed to have lived five thousand years ago. He predates the Buddha, Sankara and even Veda Vyasa.

Patanjali was the first psychologist – the West claims that position for Freud – who went deep into the problems of the mind, analysing the mind, and offering techniques to develop and tap its infinite powers. We have this great tradition of psychological investigations. The Tantra talked about the psychology of *Kundalini* power coiled at the root of the spine much before Freud talked about the "eros", the pleasure principle. If you can awaken the basic individual power and connect it to the cosmic intelligence (the Shiva *tatva*) you unfold the full potential of your person. This union creates the highest form of enery which is called Hynergy. Synergy is created when two individuals meet, i.e., your energy and my energy synergising create a new energy which is more than the two individual energies. It is like saying one plus one is three. If I keep my fingers spread out, they have very little power, but if I clench them and make my hand into a fist, my hand gains a new punch. Because the fingers together invoke each other and manifest hidden powers. Two people meeting together create a greater field of energy, and when their collective energy is hooked to Cosmic Intelligence they create a still greater energy called Hynergy. When two people stand apart fighting each other they create only Nygergy – negative energy.

Higher powers do exist in this world and by developing a certain sensitivity, an idealism, we will be able to integrate with these powers. Thus the human energies which are wasted in ordinary pursuits of pleasures and possessions – ruled by *kama*, *krodha* and *lobha* – need to be uplifted and transcended from these negativities, and joined with the higher principle. Only then is it possible to become a highly creative person.

Patanjali elaborately dwells upon the art of uplifting your

energy through various psychic centres and intergrating it with deeper and higher powers creating Synergies and Hynergies leading you to the seminal experience of a shower of bliss – *dharma megha samadhi* – from the beyond.

In quest of this higher energy – Hynergy – which is not available in our ordinary interactions, Patanjali has given various self-development schemes in the book called *Yoga Sutras*, (Sutras are small meaningful statements, and Yoga is union).

Yoga has various definitons. *Bhagavad Gita* defines yoga in the following ways:

(1) **Yoga is the pursuit of excellence.** It means that whatever we do has to be done perfectly, even if it is just the routine of fixing breakfast. We are imperfect in our work because the mind is not behind our work. **As a fist step, concentration in work is to be developed.** Don't say: "I failed in the examination and therefore want to become a yogi." A student who doesn't study well, or a businessman who is not good in his business, cannot aspire to scale new heights.

(2) **Yoga is balancing the mind – equanimity.** It is contemplation by cutting off thoughts and observing the situation in a detached manner.

(3) **Yoga is the capacity to remain rooted in your Self while you are interacting in the world.** This means that you are not upset but calm and cool under all circumstances. A person who stays rooted in yoga never feels any tiredness;

he is able to bring new energies to work – doing things in his own innovative way. The more he works, the more he is inspired, i.e., he is able to draw energy from within himself.

These are actually the three stages of yoga. The **concentration** powers are developed, then the **detachment** powers are developed and then you are able to **concentrate with detachment**. New dimensions of consciousness open up in your self, and when you are able to concentrate with contemplative detachment, you strike roots into your own inner self, which is the source of infinite energy. A yogi therefore does not need inspiration from the outside world. On the contrary he inspires the world around him.

Yoga is freedom from misery, depression or agitation which are various faces of *dukha*, the smallness of mind, the limited space you identify with. When you are free from *dukha* – pain, distress, depression, etc., – you enjoy your natural health. That is perfect yoga.

A yogi is one who can be naturally, effortlessly happy; one who does not become unhappy under pressure of the situation. **That state of natural happiness is the final achievement of the yogi**. I would call him a yogi who has the inner strength to smile all the way. Hence Bhagavan says of yoga in the *Gita*: "Yoga is not union, yoga is disunion." Disjunction from *dukha* is yoga. Then you attain your natural state as *sukha* – a vastness of space, a carefree attitude, a playfulness about oneself. When you attain that, you are a yogi.

Bhagavan Sri Krishna says that in that state of yoga infinite creativities arise. He continues "… from an infinitesimal speck of Me, I manifest the entire universe." This power to create without getting exhausted is yoga. The more you create, the more inspired and energetic you become.

Generally yoga is understood as sitting quietly and doing nothing. The idea is that he doesn't feel he is doing anything. A yogi does not even sweat (meaning he doesn't get exhausted) because he keeps that coolness of mind.

Patanjali treated yoga as a special subject and wrote the *Yoga Sutras*, of course drawing inspiration from the Upanishads and the Vedas. There are 195 sutras.

Patanjali begins – "Therefore, now, let us begin the study of yoga." Why does he say 'now'? Because, it is suggested, you have experimented with everything else, and finally have come to yoga. See the vigour and precision of the mind of Patanjali. In such a few words he has packed lot of ideas.

Then comes the definition of yoga. Patanjali says, "Yoga is restraining thought modifications, mastering the mind." We are prisoners of our thoughts; riding on thoughts we have no control over them. A thought comes to you without your permission. Instead of controlling our thoughts we have become slaves of our thoughts. It is like taking the dog for walk – wherever the dog goes you follow suit. Take the example of riding a bicycle. Over a period of time you learn how to balance, and finally you are a master of the cycle. Possession of the cycle is very important. Don't say, "I have no mastery, therefore let me do away with the cycle." You will have to then walk or crawl and you may still not reach your destination in time. The cycle is a facility given to you, but since you don't have mastery over it, the cycle becomes a burden. According to Patanjali, the mind is like that cycle. Once you accomplish controlling or mastering your mind you become your own master, you can be yourself.

Mastery over mind is a necessary precondition to discover and unfold your inner potential.

All the Vedas talk about your inner potential. They say that you are Brahman – Brahman is that which has no boundaries, no definition. It is pure intelligence, the source of all possibilities. Thus, if you can live in constant awareness of your infinite inner potential and then interact with the world, the world becomes an inspiring experience for you. The more you interact, the more your inner potential awakens. So, Patanjali says: Master your mind, gain rootedness in your self, and then interact with the world. When you achieve that, the world becomes a field for your enjoyment and a means to express your inner potential.

So far the world has been a problem for you. Mesmerised and terrorised by the world, under constant pressure you want to run away from the world and become a *sanyasi*. But *sanyasa* is not for people with that kind of "running way" attitude. The *Gita* denounces that kind of *sanyasa* as *tamasa sanyasa* (*tamasa* means idiotic). Of course you may wear the clothes of a *sanyasi* and others may respect you out of habit, but you will have no respect for yourself. Other's undeserved respect can even become a burden for you which may make you a hypocrite – pretending to be a *sanyasi* without actually being one.

True *sanyasa* is living in the constant awareness of your true Self. When that happens you will be able to interact with the world better, and the world becomes an opportunity for you to unfold your potential which is the true meaning of freedom or *moksha*, *samadhi*, yoga, or *kaivalya-bhava*. You become an integrated person unfolding your inner beauty, love, compassion, *Shiva-tatva*, or whatever you choose to call it. Yoga is not only in your aloneness; it is to be experienced in your interactions too. The way you do things, the way you handle your emotions and relationships, and your work and daily chores – all these reflect your state of yoga.

According to Patanjali, there are three fundamental factors in our life and experiences:

1. **The sensate world of objects**: the gross modification of **pradhana**, or Prakriti, is made up of three **gunas**. It is only in sleep that you don't experience the world.

2. **Mind**: which is nothing but the flow of thoughts, which you cannot avoid. According to the quality of thoughts,

your experiences change. If the mind is disturbed, the world is disturbed; if the mind is active, the world seems challenging and if your mind is peaceful you see a peaceful world. As is the mind, so is your world of experiences. No doubt there is an objective world, but the quality of mind that you bring to bear on the objective world determines the nature of your subjective experiences. Let us not blame the world for our woes and miseries, but let us blame our mind, our thought processes, for our sorrows.

According to Patanjali there is an objective world of public experience, but what the individual experiences is his subjective world of mind – the world of thoughts, feelings, and sensations.

Of course the mind can again be divided into the conscious, the subconscious and the unconscious with its individual and collective aspects. It is the unconscious which plays a decisive role in the choice and quality of thoughts.

The modern world does not cultivate and culture the mind; it is concerned with only intellectual skills and abilities. Because of this imbalance our interactions with the world cause us only sorrow.

There is a world of mind and there is a world of matter, and this mind-matter dynamics conditions our experience of the world. You can have power over matter and the world provided you have power over the mind. If you don't, the world will overpower you. The Western world also recognises the existence of mind, and the need to control the mind.

3. **Self/Individual:** Beyond the mind there is another factor in our experience, which the world of modern science is not able to accept, and that factor Patanjali calls **purusha** (the Self) – the subject. Purusha does not have any gender meaning. It only means the inner person in you, that dimension which cannot be divided. The mind interacts with the world, influences it and gets influenced by it, but the fundamental individual in you (the person), the one who owns and operates the body-mind complex interacting with the environment, is absolute. It is the ultimate goal, and not an instrument for anything beyond.

Patanjali looks upon the world as a field for the individual's self expression and enjoyment. Mind is the instrument which the individual has fashioned over many millennia.

Through a process of evolutionary interaction with the world the human being has developed this tool or, if you like, the technology, to capitalise on his experiences. Mind is the civilisational dimension of the individual. The individual interacting with nature gathers experiences and all these experiences put together become his mind. In modern economic terms, it is your social asset, or capital. It is the instrument which enhances your life.

Had there been no mind, you would have lived like a savage or an animal. In our effort to utilise that asset base, sometimes we lose our balance, and that makes us mad. The mind can either pulverise you or push you into a higher dimension of existence. It creates problems as well as opportunities. If you use the mind intelligently, it opens up opportunities. If you abuse/misuse the mind, it becomes a problem.

The modern world does not give adequate attention to the mind. Instead it gives undue attention to external capital, which is nothing but accumulated labour. Capital enhances the worth of labour. Our farmers work hard from morning till evening, but their output is very low because their work is not enhanced by the use of capital. Similarly for an animal – its productivity is low because it has no developed mind. The mind can help in our evolution but, like a ladder, it can cause our devolution also. Downfall or development, it all depends on how you use your mind.

The Purusha who works through the mind is the source of all energy and the field of infinite potential.

Patanjali identified the three factors of World, Mind and Self. But in our interaction with the world, we generally forget the Purusha, the Self, our own essential nature, and identify with either the mind or the world, losing ourselves in the process. We become slaves of the world/or of the mind which is the root cause of all humankind's problems. We have become slaves of technology and the time may not be far when all the technology is destroyed and we become helpless. Imagine a situation when you have lost all powers. Patanjali cautions the individual: "Don't forget your own inner strengths, don't live in ignorance, in total amnesia of who you are. Don't become a plaything of the forces of the world."

In the present state, we are the slaves of the world and mind, and a situation may come when mind and matter totally overpower the individual. Just as the old dinosaurs perished under their own weight, we will also perish under the weight of mind and technology.

If you forget your Self, you become a victim of mind and matter. And mind and matter have no soul. They cannot recreate themselves. How, then, can we live in constant creativity? How can we live in constant awareness of our roots so that thoughts can be planted deep in that awareness and be nourished by our own inner Self. Patanjali unfolds a scheme of thoughts moulding our world which are nourished by the Purusha, which help us continuously transcend thoughts and experiences.

The challenge for modern man is not to become a victim of, and get stuck in, his thoughts but to live in constant transcendentalism. When I create a tool, I should not become a victim of the tool. On the contrary, the tool has to be constantly upgraded and updated so that it is pliable and plastic in my hand.

It is very important that I am must live in constant awareness of my Self so that I have power over my thoughts, and am able to choose my responses to the world according to my values. This is the power that Patanjali seeks to give to man. He enunciates a simple principle – "*Chitta vrutti nirodha.*" That means controlling or mastering the thought modifications of the mind.

It should be noted that mind arises as a result of interaction with the world. Mind does not manifest itself in the absence of interactions. When I stand near a table, it neither provokes me nor do I feel threatened by the presence of the table. But when I am near another person, I look at him and he looks at me and that is the beginning of mind. The table does not objectify me, but when I look at another individual, I am objectified. In this process a new entity arises – the mind. So the mind manifests itself in relationship and so long as you nourish relationships, there is experience of the mind. Relationships are established in terms of productive work; that is, when we have something to do together. Relationships manifest themselves when there is investment in an interaction. When there is no investment in a relationship, there is no stake involved. But in a productive relationship, there is a stake and the need for dominance. Therefore, it is only in productive interactions, as we work together and invest our energy and time, that problems arise. If the mind is a product of interaction between people then how do I go back to rooting in my Self and then interact with the world?

According to Patanjali the mind has to be mastered and then your are able to abide in your Self. If that is not happening, there is every chance of getting lost in the whirlpools of the mind. When you step into the river Ganges, you have to be careful otherwise the swirling water will take you into the sea. You need something to hold onto. This is equivalent to holding on to the Self, or constant awareness of the Self and then moving into the turbulence of the mind which is interacting with the world. That holding on to the Self is possible by controlling and watching the mind. In effect, you can say: "Know and be rooted in your Self," or, "Control the mind, and then interact with the world." If you can do that then the world becomes a fantastic opportunity for you to unfold your inner potential. That is true freedom – to make your life a series of enjoyable experiences. You will then become a great worker, an accomplished producer and a well-informed consumer, which is what modern management is all about. How to go about doing this?

Patanjali gives eight steps. These are *yama*, *niyama*, *asana*, *pranayama*, *pratyahara*, *dharana*, *dhyanam*, and *samadhi*. (In *samadhi* itself he identifies nine stages: *Savitharka*, *nirvitharka*, *savichara*, *nirvichara*, *samprajnata*, *asamprajnata*, *sabeeja*, *nirbeeja* and *saheja*).

1. **Yama** (social virtues) is to be practised by one in social relationships. These virutes are honesty/truthfulness, respect for the other and universal vision. The vision is: "Do not deprive others of what legitimately belongs to them", because "all wealth belongs to all". In Patanjali's

language these virtues are: *Satya, ahimsa, brahmacharya, astheya* and *aparigraha*.

2. **Niyama** (personal virtues): These are austerity, self study, cheerfulness, purity of mind (motives and intentions) and surrender to God – Synergy with the Cosmic Intelligence.

3. **Asana** (mastery over the body): No gesture escapes you without awareness. You might have noticed that when alone, you dig your nose, dig the earth with you toe, shake your thighs, etc., which shows lack of mastery. It is a waste of energy. *Asana* is basically an ability to sit still and comfortably for about 45 minutes (*sthiram sukham asanam*).

4. **Pranayama:** This is working on your breath (*prana*) and nervous system (*nadi*) so that the whole physiological activity comes under your control. The way you breathe affects your metabolism, which has an important role in the process of aging and illness. By controlling the process of breathing you remain young and healthy.

5. **Pratyahara:** This is judgement-free watching of thoughts, and inwardness of your attention on the Self.

6. **Dharana:** Focusing the mind's attention to a limited space, or on an inspiring object or theme, which also means focusing on the light of the Self (*Chittasya desa bandhata*).

7. **Dhyana:** This means that the mind continues to abide on the chosen theme without distracting or dissimilar thoughts (*tatra pratyaya Ekatanata*).

8. **Samadhi**: This denotes the state where the experiencer disappears into the flame of experience. Only the pursuit remains, the ego is absent, which is a state of excellence. As you listen to the speaker, the speaker disappears, you disappear, and only the listening remains. You bring out your best in this state (*Swaroopa soonyamiva tateva artha mathranirbhasam*).

Samadhi itself can be perfected. That is the perfection of perfection. A state comes when you totally abide in the Self: you can choose your thoughts – quality, quantity, and direction, and also choose the quality of interaction with the world. You unfold your own essential power, self and beauty. Then the world no more remains a problem but becomes an opportunity for your self-expansion and self-expression. You become like a great musician who cradles the musical instrument (the world), runs his fingers (interacts) on the strings (situations) and brings out warbling notes of music (joy). Through the world you express the celestial music that you are capable of – your *sacchidananda* state of plenum. It is the state of dynamic meditation. In *samadhi*, or dynamic meditation, there is no difference between Prakriti and Purusha (matter and consciousness). There is total integration, and the individual enjoys *kaivalyam* (absolute oneness).

Friends, I do not have time to go into more details, but I have given you a broad outline of Patanjali's scheme of developing the personality, and integrating the world into the development of individuality. Follow the scheme till the world, the mind and the individual self become one. It is the Dance of Shiva according to Tantra, or *jeevan mukti* according to Vedanta.

The *samadhi* state is the final state unfolded in our scriptures and that is what we want to experience by rooting in our culture.

Innovativeness, Effectiveness and Competitiveness

Before I go into the topic, I would like to interact with you on the present economic situation, on the paradigm shift taking place and the change in the consciousness of human goals and the evolving solutions for our economic problems. All my responses to the economic situations are based on the vision of the *Bhagavad Gita*. The *Gita* says that spiritual evolution and material development are not contradictory phenomena. They are complementary. One can spiritually evolve and at the same time work for material development. Earlier, we thought that spiritual development or unfoldment is opposed to material development; one set of people dedicated to material progress

Talk at the All India Management Conference, Bangalore in 1994.

and another set of people dedicated to spiritual progress and the twain would never meet.

But in the present phase of economic evolution we find the outlines of a new promise, where both the goals can be pursued, where East and West can meet as I announced in the inauguration of the Research Foundation, that "God realisation is Goal realisation" When I set a goal and try to reach that goal, in the process I draw upon myself, my own inner resources, and experience the divine. The experience of the divine, or the experience of God, is a continuous experience of marching toward the goal by setting targets higher and higher. And that infinitude of your experience in its totality is God experience. So there is no fundamental difference between God experience and Goal realisation. The *Bhagavad Gita* very beautifully defines it as, "*Karmani akarmadarsanam*" – action-less action. One can remain as an actionless centre in the midst of all activity. One can draw from one's own inner recesses the energy necessary for productive and creative activities. This is the fundamental paradigm which the *Gita* tries to expound for modern problems.

Secondly, we have witnessed the death of mass ideologies and the emergence of the individual. Mass ideologies for the sake of communities, religions, and nationalities have been overtaken. Now the need is to shift the attention to the development of the individual. It is not ideology that is important but the contentment and happiness of the individual which is more important. That kind of a paradigm shift has taken place in the modern world.

Thirdly, there is an increasing awareness of the invisible costs of economic development – like ecological degradation and psychological disintegration of the individual. Though we have achieved incredible progress in the economic field, at the same time we have damaged the ecology and environment in which we are living. In our economic development, we must take into consideration the ecological problem and also the psychological problems of individuals. In the process of creating wealth how is a human being treated? What is the quality of a successful manager? Quantity is easy to measure. He commands so much salary. He has got a palatial house. He has got the longest car in the world, a custom-made car, and he wears only custom-made suits. He flies in his private jet. But what is the quality of the life of the individual? We need to ask a different set of questions. Some of them are: Is he leading a contented, creative, harmonious life? Or is he leading a life of inner rottenness? What is the quality of his family life? How does he treat his children and his wife? How does he behave with his servants? What is the general quality of his life?

The inner integrity of the individual, the happiness of the individual, is important. Unless we take into consideration these aspects in our calculation of progress, we will not be able to measure true progress. This is another trend we are increasingly witnessing. We will not congratulate a person simply because he has got the biggest house in the city unless his quality, mind, behaviour and inner enjoyment also merit admiration.

Economic progress can ensure creature comforts to the entire humanity, if not today, tomorrow. We see a glimmer of hope on the distant horizon. A stage has come which can ensure creature comforts to all. When I say creature comforts – I mean comfortable housing, good food, medical facilities and education. Earlier, it was not possible. In an agrarian society it wasn't possible. In a pre-industrial society it wasn't possible. But in modern society, we find that the logical end of capitalist progress is comfort for all. It is a consumer-driven economy. It is a market-oriented economy. A stage has come where we can ensure at least minimum comforts to the entire population of the world.

Fourthly, in our efforts to develop, we find two kinds of societies – the developed and developing. Among the developed countries, what was the method of development? For the development of their economies, European nations exploited a section of deprived citizens of the same country. Capital formation was through exploitation. That kind of exploitative capital-oriented development, whether it is by resource exploitation or by enslaving a section of one's own population, is now not possible. It is not possible because the entire humanity has awakened to a new dawn of hope and prosperity. For India it is neither possible for us to colonise a nation, nor is it possible to enslave a section of the people in our own country because we are living in a free world.

What, then, we might ask could be the new method of development? Have we missed the historic opportunity for development? Fortunately we have found a new method of development. It is export-oriented development: Export, earn foreign exchange and then purchase capital goods and upgrade the quality of your population. Through this process Taiwan, Indonesia, Japan, Korea have all experienced economic development. It is a kind of export-driven economic development, not the colony-driven or slave-driven capital formation and economic growth. So for capital formation we don't have to have colonies. We don't have to have a section of the population enslaved and exploited. Neither do we need exploitation of children, nor exploitation of farmers. We can still accumulate capital, which we have done. We have opened our economy. Our foreign exchange reserves have gone up from one billion to 20 billion dollars [62 billion at the turn of the century]. With this we can command latest technologies.

In the export-driven economy, it is important to add value to your product. We cannot export all kind of manufactured goods and compete with developed countries. We cannot export cars in competition with America, Germany or Japan. We cannot compete with Korea and Japan in shipbuilding. So we have to identify our own areas. The crux is a value-added economy and not a simple manufacturing or a simple agricultural economy. And in value-adding productive activity what is important is human resource development. Of course land development is important and so is infrastructural development. But what is more important and pivotal, or the core area, is human resource development. To add value you must create vision. You must have an idea. Isn't it? You pick up a rusted piece of iron from the street. For an ordinary person it has no value. You take it, you put it in the fire and when it is glowing red hot, you place it on an anvil and beat it into shape and make a blade out of it. You think that just the blade is not sufficient. You make some carvings on it. Then you fix a handle to it. Then you think that this also is not sufficient and you put some teeth to the blade. Now you have a first class knife. A scrap of iron which was lying valueless on the road can now command value. To a basic resource, to the raw material, you have added value. Meaningless on the road, it has become meaningful adorning your dining table. Now it has got a value. Or take a sculptor. He picks up a piece of stone and chips off unnecessary parts and then he makes a beautiful idol and he sells it in the market. This is what I mean by value-adding by creating visions and ideas and turning those visions into products and services.

Creating visions and ideas is possible when you can invoke your inner energy. It is not exploitation which spurs modern economic development, but an inner exploration. Individuals must explore themselves. Such individuals have to be encouraged.

I would call them entrepreneurs or leaders of the economy. They can be called leaders, entrepreneurs, facilitators, whatever name you give them. They are not looking outside for inspiration, they are looking inward for their inspiration. They will not blame anybody for their situation. They will make use of any situation for their growth. Such people can give a drive and push to economic activities. They are able to look inward and create their values. They are to be identified and encouraged; they must be nourished.

Let us say that such people of leadership qualities constitute from 3 to 10 per cent of the population. They are the true leaders of the country.

It is usually such people who are interested in knowing what is effectiveness, what is innovativeness and what is competitiveness. The others are not interested because they always want to run away from problems. They always want to blame somebody else. The leader looks inward, thinks along positive lines, and always says "I can". That is the definition of positive thinking. When a challenge comes, "Can you do that?" the response is, "Yes I can." Such people do not think parochially but think globally.

Global consciousness is not a narrow parochial national consciousness. This 10 per cent of the people are those who think globally, who want to be global leaders, who want to put their organisation into global leadership. They are not competing in the Indian market, that competitiveness is not sufficient. They must be in the cutting edge of economic activity. This set of people and a few organisations think in terms of global leadership. They think in terms of competing with Japanese companies, not some miserable company in Malabar. You are trying to compete with global leaders. Let us imagine that only globally ambitious people can have an interest in the three values we are talking about today – innovativeness, effectiveness and competitiveness.

I see in front of me a set of people who are thinking globally, who want global leadership, and who want to create an organisation which is globally competitive. It is such people that we address here. You may not belong to that category but let us dream, at least dream, together for one day. That dream doesn't cost anything, and it is from such dreams that great ideas and impossible achievements become possible.

So here we have a set of people whose ideas and ambitions are global. The next question is "Is it possible?" We have to think that it is possible. Friends, you may be interested to know that there is a new book, *Clash of Civilizations*, written by Samuel Huntington. He is a strategic thinker and visualises what the world will look like after 20, 40 or 50 years. He has identified certain general trends in the world. He says that four civilisations are competing for world supremacy. And they are the Confucian civilisation represented by China, Japan and so on; the Anglo-Saxon civilisation represented by Britain and America; the Jewish civilisation, and the Hindu, i.e., Indian, civilisation. Let us be clear that when we say Hindu it has no religious connotation. It has only a cultural connotation.

Why does he take these four civilisations? Because they have got certain general characteristics. The Chinese are spread all over the world. There are about 50 million (five crores) Chinese outside China. They are generally spread in Hong Kong, Singapore, America, the nerve centres of world economic activities. And their total wealth is 400 billion dollars, two times India's GDP. So the Chinese have got a global reach. They control, or they are going to control, Hong Kong and Singapore. They command 400 billion dollars for investment. So, too, the Jewish people. There are six million Jewish people outside Israel. They command 800 billion dollars, double that owned by the Chinese. They are known as the diaspora. Then come the Anglo-Saxon, the English speaking people. They also are spread in America, England, Australia, Singapore and so on. Wherever there are financial activities, the English-speaking people are involved. So too the Hindus. There are about 30 million Hindus outside India. They command 300 billion dollars. They are all the diaspora. We find them all over world.

It is these four sets of people who are competing for world dominance. They are fighting in the financial sector, and in the value-added sector. Most of the American research institutions are dominated by Indians who create values for them. They innovate things. If this is clear, we are no lesser people. We are on the cutting edge of world competition. It is only in India that we feel that we do not amount to anything.

Therefore, if this is true, the answer to the question, "Is it possible?" should be, "Yes, it is possible." We can capture world leadership. The twenty-first century belongs to India. This is what Huntington says. And he is from one of the leading strategic institutes of America. We don't have the confidence, but others have that confidence in us. They say that India is a sleeping gaint. When we wake up, we will realise it. Therefore they say, "Keep the giant sleeping. Inflict as many wounds as possible on him. Drug him. Confuse him." That is their strategy. But we are realising our potential and importance now.

In this context, when each one of you thinks of global leadership, you take upon yourself the responsibility for initiating economic activities, and you also look into yourself for inspiration, vision and values. It is in this context, that we come to the three important values that individuals and organisations should cultivate in their own work culture – innovativeness, effectiveness and competitiveness.

Innovativeness

How do you become an innovative person? What is innovativeness? It is adding something new to the product to create a quality which responds to human needs. Innovativeness is doing things in different ways. And for that innovativeness, where should we go? Should we read a few books? Will that make us innovative? Should we constitute a committee for creating innovative ideas? You know that when several heads were put together to draw a monkey it looked rather like a donkey! They may have ideas, but they were not able to put things integrally.

Creative impulses arise in the individual human mind and not in a collection of minds. A collective mind can make only a resolution, the lowest common denominator. It cannot scale or discover the highest peak of human intelligence. Of course you may require a kind of society, a kind of education, certain incentives, etc., but rest assured that the glimmer of creative impulse arises in the individual mind. Creativity cannot be a collective product.

Where do we look for innovativeness? Where do we look for ideas? According to Vedanta, you look toward your own self. You have got a deep unconscious mind which is a repository or treasure chest of your innumerable past experiences. From time immemorial, you have been collecting experiences. Think of diamonds. The tropical forests, may be due to an earthquake or forest fire, were buried under great pressure and finally they became diamonds. The chemical composition of both is carbon, but through heat and pressure a great transmutation took place. To discover the diamond you have to excavate the earth. You have to first prospect for and identify the diamond deposits. In the same way your unconscious mind is a treasure chest of diamonds. You have wonderful ideas. But to discover them you have to probe deep into your self. There are plenty of ideas untapped within you. They can be discovered, let us say, by keeping close to your soul, by going within your self through meditation, or through *pranayama*. Various exercises are given to move into yourself, to your inner resources, and to think in an unstructured way. The answer therefore is, "Remain close to yourself, go deep into your self, mediate, think in an unstructured fluid manner." Then you will be able to become a creative person. That is the way to innovate, or to discover, or to cultivate creativity at the top level of leadership.

Effectiveness

The second quality that we look for is effectiveness. Now let us suppose you have got wonderful ideas, or you have got beautiful training from one of the top institutions – the Massachusetts Institute of Technology, or Harvard, or the Ahmedabad Institute of Management. The left side of your brain is beautifully developed. You have got very structured, mathematical, very precise and concise thinking. And if you are put in controlled conditions you can create wonders. Don't we say in science, "Everything remaining the same, this process will produce the desired result". But the trouble with human life is that nothing remains the same. The left side of your brain is developed, your thinking is very structured, you can logically argue, you can put ideas together. But the right side of your brain, which is the seat of passion, emotions, fear, anger, insecurity and so on, is not developed. It is common experience that we have no control over our passions or our emotions.

Suppose you dislike your colleague in the office. Your reaction will be, "I don't want to sit near him." The very sight of him is enough to make you go berserk because you are not able to control your emotions – your anger, your jealousies, your small-mindedness – or to overcome your basic fears which you developed when you were moving in the jungle as you once were and you were afraid of everything. Those basic fears are still embedded in your unconscious, and they sometimes surface. When you find another healthy person you get scared – "He may hit me." When you find another beautiful person, you are afraid that everybody will look at him. When you encounter another intelligent person, you get scared. So, anybody can put that fear in you.

And you know that once you are emotionally upset all that you have learnt becomes futile. You are a very good driver, let us say. And you are driving to your office. The road is well paved and clear. There are no potholes or manholes. And the traffic lights are not working so you don't have to stop anywhere. But that particular day you can't drive. Your hands start shaking. Why? Because you had a quarrel with your wife and she gave you an ultimatum – "Either do this, or when you come home I will not be here to give you a cup of tea. You may ring up my father." You happen to be a young man, just married. If you had been married for 20 years, you may not have cared! On such a day will you be able to drive? Will you be able to concentrate on your research work? Will you be able to meditate and go deep into your self?

Therefore, unless we have a method of organising and controlling emotions, of keeping emotions under check, all the abilities and skills that we have mastered and developed through strenuous training will be of no use to us. You may be a very efficient person, a skilled person, but you will not be an effective person. The reason is because you are not able to get along with people. It is people who provoke ancient fears in you. It is people who provoke ancient anxieties in you. When I stand near a table I am not afraid of the table. It doesn't make me self-consciousness. It doesn't create any emotional upsurge in me. I can sit and do my work. But when my colleague comes and sits near me, all my ancient fears are awakened. My boss can upset me, my subordinates can upset me, my friends can upset me, my enemies can upset me. In an office you can expect these four categories of people. You cannot avoid them. You will have a boss. Can you avoid him? And you will have enemies also. I am sure each one of you must have at least one enemy. And when you see him, your blood pressure goes up. Your stomach is upset. You may have butterflies in your stomach. You don't know what to do.

Unless you are able to keep your attention on the goal and manage such emotional *rakshasas* coming and attacking you,

you will not be able to move toward the realisation of your goal. Having set a goal, do not allow emotions and ancient fears to interfere in realising the goal. The capacity to realise the goal is called effectiveness. You should not say "No, I am hurt. I am humiliated. My wife is sick, my child is sick. I do not know what do." Never allow these emotions to continue. Have a certain control over your emotions. I don't say you will not be afraid. There can be fear. There can be anxiety. But all these should be under control. So, to be an effective person, not only do you require the development of the left side of your brain – the techniques, skills and technologies – but you also need a certain culturing of the right side of your brain which is the seat of your emotions and ancient fears.

In all our training programmes, we must have a programme for developing, controlling and mastering emotions. Let me emphasise that emotions are very important. They give a certain drive to your pursuits. If you are not an emotional person you will not get the drive. If you are not rational you will not get a direction. We need both: the drive and the direction. We *need* the drive. An extra magazine of energy can be given only by emotions and passions. If you are not a passionate person, then there is no drive. There should be certain fire in your life. If that is not there, you will sit down like a question mark, weighed down by dejection, or like a cynical person questioning everything. Rather like your grand uncle who has nothing to do. He sits with a newspaper, and whatever you may say, he will say, "No."

Emotions and passions give you a certain drive, a certain extra impetus. Without that you cannot reach the ultimate goal. You will hover somewhere in the middle. At the same time, without reasoning and certain technological knowledge and rational capacities, you will not be able to gain a direction. Emotion without direction is blind. Direction without passion is lame.

For modern managers we need neither the lame or the blind. We need people with all limbs intact. We need a certain culturing of emotions rather than the elimination of emotions and passions. If any religious man tells you to curb and destroy your emotions and become like a "dry stump of tree" tell him, " I am not for that, Sir. I want to become a flowering tree full of foliage and flowers which glisten in the morning sun. I want to become a tree to which the clouds can sing and the birds can come for rest, not a dry stump of a tree which somebody will cut and put in the fire."

So, a certain culturing and nourishing of your emotions is necessary. When there is the harmonious development of your passion and reason, the right and left sides of your brain, then you become a balanced person. In *Bhagavad Gita* this is known as the state of yoga, which is the balance of passion and reason. With such balance you can become an effective person. Thereafter, you will not be perturbed when somebody provokes you, when your peon does not salute you, or your wife doesn't remember your birthday. These are the usual causes of quarrels. You might react like Arjuna did, "Why should I work? I am going to become a sanyasi and go to the ashram." But that is not the solution as Krishna explained. You will carry the same mind to the ashram also. There too you will find something to complain about: "He did not give me fruit." If you carry the same mind there, you will be the same wretched person.

Wherever you are, what is important is the development of the left and the right sides of your brain. Give passion to your reason and give reason to your passion. Then alone can you be an effective person.

Competitiveness

We have seen that a global leader should be effective and innovative. The third quality envisaged by global leadership is competitiveness. The competitive spirit has to be maintained in all fields – in the quality of the product, cost and services. Today, we have to maintain competitiveness on a global level. When we say competitiveness, it is not a competition with weaklings. We are not talking about competition with your neighbour. What is needed is a global competitiveness. We have to set very high standards. We must have our own standards. And it is essential to reinvent the standards to be maintained everytime, based on global standards.

If we want to compete in the world as an organisation, we

have to have our own self-set standards. Competitiveness out of envy is destructive competitiveness, which is *matsarya buddhi*. It will not do any good either for oneself or for the country. Competitiveness means you are competing with yourself. You constantly explore your potential and limits. Take, for example, Japan and the Japanese slogan of "zero-defect". Zero defect was the standard they aimed at. To reach this standard they had to make continuous improvements. Japanese called this the *kaisen*. It is a continuous, but incremental improvement, in contrast to sudden bursts which was the habit of Europeans and Americans.

Both as a country and as individuals we have to think globally and we have to constantly expand our limits. Then alone is high performance possible. Friends, I think that if at least a few leaders can take up this challenge, our country will emerge as a Super Power in the world.

On Leadership Values

When a minister, new to the post, proposes utopian schemes to uplift the poor by providing them free cloth and food, the well-experienced bureaucrat will retort that such things are not possible. "We don't have the resources, nor do we have the manpower." Thus, he exercises certain caution and control over the dream of that young minister.

Our respected Chief Secretary spoke similarly the other day. However, when he said Peter denied Christ three times, he might have forgotten the fact that it was that same Peter who helped establish the solid foundation on which the church has

Presidential address on the occasion of The Inauguration of Bodhananda Research Foundation for Management and Leadership studies (BRFML) at Thiruvanthapuram on 21.1.1994.

been built, a foundation which is still strong and the church has an adherence of more than one billion people in this world. When the Chief Secretary said that   na forgot the lessons, he was forgetting the fact that it wa. the same Arjuna who fought the battle of *Mahabharata* and won. He thus helped the Lord to establish the rule of law and *dharma*.

Let us not have a blinkered outlook like the bureaucrat. Let us not sink into the syndrome of seeing the thorns and missing the flowers. Let us not share the pessimistic attitude which prevails in this country today. But in our enthusiasm to build the country on a firm footing we shouldn't miss the impediments and obstacles, and the practical considerations involved in building the new, solid foundation. There are impediments and one should be aware of them. If one is not aware of them, one will not be able to build. Rome was not built in a day. As we go ahead with our plans and schemes, we may have to re-evaluate, re-adjust, re-invent, re-engineer and then go ahead. It is not as simple as setting a goal once and then blindly rushing toward it. One must be cautious at every step.

I think that there are two lessons for us. The first is that we should not be like the bureaucrat, seeing only obstacles – the "buts" and "ifs" – whenever a new idea is proposed. The second lesson is that one has to be very cautious. One has to know what are the impediments.

When people do not put things in the proper perspective,

and draw wrong conclusions, employing a wrong methodology it becomes very painful. The *Bhagavad Gita* is not mainly speaking about death as the bureaucrat would have us believe. The *Gita's* main teaching is the deathlessness of the spirit. That the born shall die, and the dead shall be reborn, is only a supplementary teaching. And it is only when you don't understand the immortal soul, that the Lord touches upon the mortal aspects of existence. If the Devil reads the Bible, it becomes very difficult, unless you put things in perspective.

Today we are discussing essentially the management problems, and we will have occasion to refer to the *Bhagavad Gita* which, when properly understood, has much wisdom to offer.

When we try to reflect on today's problems, and on why we are having a management institute, the first thing we realise is that the world is becoming one space. We are not talking in a smaller or a narrow, parochial context. We are not talking as a Malayali. We are not talking as even an Indian. We are talking as a world citizen. Unless that context is clear, this dialogue will not be meaningful. We find that ideological walls are crumbling. We find that national walls are being lowered. We find that religious fences are being removed. All these differences, walls and fences, are coming down or are being demolished and there is a free flow of ideas, capital, technology, talent, products, etc. We are living in an environment where the world is becoming, increasingly, one economic space. I hope you will agree with me. The crumbling of the ideological walls is represented by the demolition of the Berlin wall, in 1991. Again we saw walls crumbling down when (the late) Israeli Prime Minister Yitzhak Rabin shook hands with Hussain, the King of Jordan, across the Jordan river. In the late 1970s we found the then US President Richard Nixon going to China, standing by the Great Wall and beaming his avuncular smile to the world. The world is becoming smaller, and it will be one economic space. This has to be accepted.*

I don't say that the entire world population has moved into that space. But people who count, people who matter – people who take decisions for others – those people have moved into that space. The 20 per cent of world population who take decisions, who are articulate and whose views matter, who move men and material in this world, are moving into that economic space. Let us accept that fact. Today I will be speaking from that standpoint. Let us not think only as Malayalis, even though we are essentially Malayalis, rooted in Kerala. But we have to grow, and our branches have to touch the heavens and hold a dialogue with the stars and the sun. Then alone will our being rooted here have some meaning. Let us not lie low and remain closed. Let us open up ourselves. Let us strike roots deep into the soil, but let us touch the heavens too. It is with that spirit that we are standing here today. We conceive the purpose of

*In the last decade the European Union, comprising of 15 countries has grown stronger and in 2001 introduced a common currency, the Euro.

the Trust to be in this direction.

We will register this Trust in Thiruvanthapuram and will have regional centres in all metropolitan cities and in emerging metros such as Bangalore, Hyderabad and Ahmedabad. We will have regional centres and patrons from industrial houses and we will organise research studies, offer seminars, develop a nine-member faculty. This nine-member faculty will be well versed both in modern management theories and scriptures. There will be a kind to synergy between these two disciplines.

We are going to be a giant experiment in the field of management and leadership studies, integrating our ancient Vedantic values with modern needs. But let us consider where we stand now.

Firstly there is the homogeneity of economic space. The second thing I find is that ideologies are dead. Earlier people were fighting for ideologies: "I am a communist", "You are Congress", "I am a Muslim", "You are a Christian", "I am a Chinese", "You are a Russian", "I am an Indian," "You are a Pakistani" and so on. The clashes were all on an imaginary ideological plane. Now we find that all those ideological clashes are disappearing. The clash has increasingly become economic. It is an economic war. Japan is trying to export more. America is trying to export more. The new economic tigers, the South East Asian nations, are trying to export more. The war is thus increasingly becoming intellectual rather than physical. The war is being fought in terms of products and movement of products, rather than by the movement of armies, tanks and aeroplanes.

This has to be understood. Whoever produces low-cost quality goods, and exports more, will dominate the world. That is why America feels threatened, even though they have enough military muscle. America, a nation of 30 crores of people, is afraid of a small country such as Japan with just 11 crores of people. They are afraid of Japan not because Japan has superior military power but because of their superior productivity.

If you want to operate on the global level, you have to take into account these changes. And I tell you if you don't think in global terms but only in regional parochial terms, then you will be finished. You will be floating like dust in the world. You have to think in terms of global initiative. You have to be a global competitior, not just a competitor between Malabar and Travancore, or between Cochin and Travancore.

We have to enlarge our thinking and vision. The best in this country must think in terms of the global context, global competitiveness, not a local competitiveness. That is why the name of the Foundation includes "Leadership studies". We are addressing the leaders of this country. The leader cannot be a second-rate leader. Earlier, if you wanted to be a leader, you could be the leader of a small area. Today, television is bringing information, satellites are bringing ideas from all over the world instantly. Being a small panchayat president here means nothing.

If you want to be a leader, you must be a global leader. You must command a global corporation.

When we use the term "Management and Leadership Studies" we are addressing that quality of leadership here. I am not addressing the masses here. I am not trying to rabble-rouse the masses. I am trying to appeal to the leadership impulses in a few people, people who care for excellence, quality, initiative and competitiveness. I am addressing those people. Think of a train carrying dozens and dozens of bogies. How many engines are there? One engine in the front and one engine at the back. Because of the engines the whole train moves. Likewise, if we can inspire 10 per cent of leadership quality in this country, then our purpose in initiating this organisation will have been served.

We *have* to think of commanding leadership on a global level in the economic field. And leadership means leadership in economic activities because all wars have been reduced to an economic war. Earlier we used to fight with fists. Then we fought with arrows, then with guns. Later we started fighting with missiles. Now we have started fighting with thoughts, ideas and visions. That is the level of war going on in the world today.

If this is also understood that the world is becoming one economic space, that the wars are on an economic plane then what is important is leadership. If the leader is a quality leader, he can inspire the whole people. Earlier, we thought that the masses can be uplifted. The Communists tried that in Russia; they tried to uplift the entire population and we know how miserably they failed. Communism was a great ideal but it became a colossal failure.

The new thinking now is that we will not be able to uplift the entire mass all of a sudden. We have to create areas of excellence. The economic development in certain zones in China is 40 per cent per year, while all other areas are dragging behind. But they know that once you inspire one area, then all other areas will have a role model. They will definitely follow suit. So it is with the 'tiger' nations – Singapore or Korea or Taiwan. They are all small nations following that pattern of development. Now we are not trying, like the Communists tried, to uplift the entire population. We are trying to target our development activities. We are trying to identify areas, identify people, identify such economic activities with which we are comfortable, and in which we enjoy a competitive advantage. It is a targeted development. It is a development through leaders. It is development by entrepreneurs. It is developing the elite of this country. I may seem a little orthodox and capitalistic in my proposition, but I cannot help it. We have to identify and develop an elite section of the society and concentrate on leadership qualities and initiatives. In turn they will uplift the population.

From that standpoint, we find that it is the middle class of this country who can provide leadership. They are going to be the engines of Indian development, not the 80 percent of the poor people. So we have to concentrate upon the elites, the leaders, the middle class. This is a Capitalist mode of development. The cat is out of the bag! What we are saying is that a Capitalist mode of development is where excellence, leadership and initiatives are identified and encouraged.

If such leaders are necessary, if such initiatives are necessary, how do we go about it? Now, I hope there is a consensus that the whole world is becoming one economic space; battles are fought on economic terms; we have to develop leadership; and it is those leaders who are points and centres of excellence who will uplift this country. That is the experience of Indonesia. That is the experience of Taiwan. That is the experience of Korea and Japan. If you try to develop the entire population, it will be a colossal failure, which has been the experience of Russia. China very intelligently understood this midway and quietly changed its strategy of development.

At the same time, it must be asked if in our programme for economic development, we are going to emulate the West blindly? There are two problems in the Western mode of development. One is the ecological problem, the other is their experience of various psychological problems. In the process of creating wealth, the one who creates the wealth becomes the first casualty. You must have seen a very rich man who owns a lot of property, but who is inwardly poor. He is sick. He is diabetic. His heart has failed several times. He has every conceivable psychological and physical problem. He has visited hospitals several times. And still he owns wealth. His family life is in utter disarray. He has not seen his grand-children. He has not seen his children for several weeks, because he was busy visiting different countries. So there is a family problem. The invisible cost of development is in terms of ecology and psychology. Therefore, we have to introduce a new modus operandi, a new way of development, where these factors are taken into consideration.

Modern management has accepted the primacy of the individual as the most important factor. It is not money. It is not the machine. It is not technology. All these, some how or the other, we can procure. What is important is the development of the individual, the happiness of the individual. After all, of what use is this economic development if the individual is unhappy? Modern man has created all kinds of comforts, but inside he is very very unhappy – comfortably unhappy, of course! He is not a happy person. He is not an integrated person. He is not able to unfold his potential completely.

Therefore, modern management concentrates upon the development of the individual, the happiness of the individual. Developed countries are known as life-style economies. In the ordinary Capitalist mode of development, they think about the consumption needs of the individual. But in Japan they have now started thinking about the total quality of the individual as a producer and as a consumer. Is the individual happy? Is he happy in participating in the productive activties of the country? Is he happy as a consumer? Ultimately, the test of the success of economy is the intergrity, happiness and development of the individual.

In the *Bhagavad Gita* the concern is about individual development. I find a convergence between the individual trying to develop himself and the development of the economy. Earlier, economic development was always based on the exploitation of the individual and natural resources. If you study our history of economic development there was exploitation of resources and raw materials to produce goods and services, or the exploitation of labour. This is how the Capitalist economies grew. Either they exploited vast colonies, or they exploited their own labour force. But resources are scarce. We are experiencing that now. And the labourer is a free person. You can no longer exploit the labourer. He is highly conscious. There are trade unions. There is a constitution. He is a citizen of a free country. If you ask him to work for 18 hours, he is not going to accept that. So development through exploitation of labour is not possible.

How, then, do we develop? If we look at the American economy, 60 per cent of their GDP comes from value-added products and services, not from manufactured goods, nor from agricultural products. Agricultural products constitute only six per cent of their GDP. Manufactured goods constitute only

25 per cent of their GDP. What are these gun-shot jeans? You buy ordinary jeans from the local market, shoot at them to make holes and then sell them as gun-shot jeans. The jeans which you bought from the market cost only sixty rupees and you sell the gun-shot jeans for three hundred rupees. This is known as value-addition. It is a concept that you are selling. It is an idea that you are selling and not a gross product.

The modern developmental process is driven by exports. "Export or get exterminated" is the new slogan. If you want to develop, you have to export. There is no other way. It is only by exports and increasing your Forex reserves, that you can import high quality machineries and technologies so that you can increase the quality of your production. And that is possible only when you export more. You cannot get money by exporting raw material. If you export iron ore what will you get? Or rice? The best export now-a-days are Swamis. They are exported and they can bring in a lot of money. The Swami is not selling any 'thing.' He is selling a concept. He is selling an idea, a value-added product.

Therefore, to export we must add value. Unless you create a new idea and sell it, you cannot command foreign reserves.

How do we create ideas? What is the source of the ideas? What is the source of the idea of gun-shot jeans? One man, one fine morning, thought about it. And he saw that we were initially living in the forests for a long period. After that we had an agricultural economy for 6,000 years. And then for the past 300 years we have been experiencing the industrial economy. The experiences of those initial years are embedded in our unconscious. All those years we had been hunting animals, puncturing their hides. Remove the hide, and you get an arrow-shot hide. We had been wearing that. Our unconscious had a secret desire for such things. And somebody discovered that. He was convinced that gun-shot jeans could be sold. It would have a subliminal attraction for the youth. That is how he discovered it. And it is being sold. So it is not natural resource or labour which is important in the modern export-driven developmental strategy. What is important is ideas, visions and values. And where do ideas, visions and values come from? They come from the human recesses; they come from the soul of human beings.

To get ideas and values, there is no point in reading books. There is no point in discussions. One has to go inward. One has to go deep into one's own self. When one goes deep into one's own self, he gets new ideas and those ideas can be customised and can be sold. Such ideas are infinite. That is what the *Bhagavad Gita* says – "O Arjuna! *Tattvamasi.*" Bhagavan says that your Self is infinite. It has got infinite ideas. You have to sit down and reflect a minute and invoke those ideas creatively. When you invoke ideas creatively, you can create a better product and you can command the world market. Ideas being infinite, there is no question of exploiting an individual. It is a question of exploring the individual and exploding his inner being in products and services.

Modern economic development will not take place by the exploitation of one individual by another, but through the exploration by every individual of his own self and bringing out those ideas. That exploration is important. I find there is a connection between the unfoldment of the individual and the unfoldment of modern economy. That is how we connect the *Bhagavad Gita* with modern economic development. Generally, people say and feel that economic development is contrary or antagonistic to spiritual development. It is a lie.

Economic development and spiritual development were antagonistic only because we were looking outward for growth. Now there is a convergence between the development and unfoldment of the individual and the development and unfoldment of the economy. There is no question of exploiting other individuals or natural resources. With minimum natural resources you can have a very rich economy, which is the experience of Japan, Israel, etc. That is the experience of Switzerland, too, where there are not many big industries, but only small-scale, household industries. They command one of the biggest economies. Their per capita income is, perhaps, a hundred times more than India's.

It is possible to unfold your potential and contribute to economic development. Perhaps I should say, God-realisation is Goal-realisation. Set an economic goal and as you unfold and march toward that goal you experience God. God-experience occurs while you interact with your environment; you are unfolding and invoking your inner spirit in terms of ideas and values, and you give shape to a product and service. Thus you can continuously experience economic development in terms of self-unfoldment.

Friends, let us not see any contradiction between these two pursuits. When you think on those lines you realise that the *Bhagavad Gita* and our spiritual literature has so much to contribute. Our scriptures – the *Gita*, *Mahabharata*, Upanishads – talk about the inner being of the individual which is the source of all productivity, of all visions, ideas and values. Through meditation, or various other psychic and spiritual disciplines, you will be able to invoke the recesses of your own inner being and become a creative and productive person. Productivity, creativity and spiritual sadhana are not contradictory but are complementary.

The thought of the unity between spiritual and material pursuits guided us and inspired us to establish the Research Foundation for Management and Leadership Studies. Human society has developed to such a state where you can harmonise these two pursuits, to invoke incessantly from the individual being who can be continuously creative in his interactions with the world. We are addressing only the leaders of this country in various fields of activity, not the masses. We will try to educate the leaders in our scriptures – the *Bhagavad Gita*, Upanisads, *Mahabharata*, *Ramayana*, Brahmasutras,

Manusmrti, Panchatantra, *Yogasutras*, Nyayasastras, etc. The entire wealth of Indian spiritual and cultural literature will be placed at the disposal of the modern leaders. They will interact with it. They will accept whatever is necessary. We expect to kindle a creative interaction between the Rishi and the manager, between our old traditions and modern management needs.

Thank you very much.

3

Mind

Man stands out from animals because of his mind. Mind is the faculty which receives stimuli from the outer world, and responds to those stimuli by an evolutionary impulse, conditioned by past experiences, and by an inborn urge to survive.

The mind can become a means for self-unfoldment, or for self-aggrandisement, setting off forces of harmony and love or, on the contrary, forces of disharmony and hatred. It is a powerful tool, through sharpening which one can understand the mystery of existence, or by neglecting which one becomes a victim of circumstances.

Right understanding, right work attitudes, and meditation help the mind to self-organise and invoke the eternal sources of creative energy and true happiness.

Churning for Management Values

Incredible changes are taking place in the economic space of our country. I call them tumultuous changes. We are moving away from a command, centralised economy to a decentralised market economy. The decision-making process is changing. Ten years ago, the Planning Commission used to be the centre of the decision-making process. Now, the centre of decision-making is the market place governed by market forces. The government is abjuring its responsibility, rightly so, and the various corporations of the country are taking over the responsibility of deciding what resources go into what kind of production and how the growth of the nation is to be targeted. Our economy is opening up; it

Talk at Torrent-AMA Management Centre, Ahmedabad, in 1993.

is opening to the influences of world economies, the world's market forces. We are keeping the windows of our economy open. We are doing this with a trembling heart because we are not sure of ourselves. But our rishis said once upon a time: "Let noble thoughts come from all sides," meaning, "Let us not be afraid of outside influences, let thoughts come from all sides." I think, therefore, the opening up process is good for us. We will know where we lack, what our strengths and weaknesses are so that the pluses and minuses can be understood and an objective evaluation becomes possible. Also, there can be an effective interaction between views, ideas and products. This is the environment in which we are operating.

Therefore, we need a new management style as we see that the politicians have abdicated their responsibility – they no more think that they can lead this country; they no more think that they can create ideas for our economy. Once upon a time Mahatma Gandhi and other politicians used to do that. They used to create ideas, organise people and inspire them to undertake the right activities, but the politician of today, because of his moral depravity, has lost his faith and courage to do this. The managers, the technocrats, the economists, the intelligentsia of this country, have to take up this responsibility. There is no point in anyone blaming the politicians. Let us not look up to them; let us look up to the technocrats of this country. It is our responsibility therefore to take courage in our hands and create visions, ideas and translate them into products and services, so that we can command a prestigious position in the comity of nations in the world market. This is the situation in which we are sitting together here and trying to listen to the voice of the ancient masters. I don't say I will be able to put across their ideas as well as they should be, but whatever I have learnt and whatever I have understood and whatever of this has been beneficial to me, I will put across.

Since we are opening up, it is very important that the Indian leaders – and I would call you all leaders: the Indian managerial class, the businessmen, the technocrats, entrepreneurs – all must have a deep knowledge of the Indian scriptures, the Indian ethos, in the same way as we have heard that America has got a management style, or that Japan has got a management style of their own, a style of getting things done, organising things, conceiving products, etc. Nowadays they talk about civilisational confrontation. It is not true that corporations are conflicting or confrontationist but it is nations which are competing. Recently I read an article in *The Times of India* that said: "Unless we sell India, we can't sell an Indian product, an Indian brand." Unless we have confidence in our country, our culture, our way of life, our way of looking and experiencing things, we will not be able to sell our products. It is very important that we must know who we are, where our strengths lie and what are our weaknesses. So, from that standpoint, to formulate a new management philosophy and system we have to go back to our culture so that we can participate in this so called civilisational confrontation.

Are there are any books or texts which expound the Indian view and way of life? Is there any one textbook? For example, for the Anglo-Saxon culture, there is the Bible. Let us say the Bible is the fundamental source of values which conditioned their way of looking at life and experiencing life. In my view, the Western civilisation conquered the whole world with the help of the Bible. Science, technology, organisation came later. First they created an environment of respect for Western culture with the help of the Bible. It is said that when the Christians went to Africa they had the Bible and the Africans had the land, and after 200 years, the Africans got the Bible and the Europeans got the land. Exchange had taken place. I am not criticising them; that is the way of the world. It was a cultural invasion which paved the way for the ideological and economic invasion. So, unless we culturally prepare our people, psychologically prepare them, we are not going to sell ourselves or be competitive in the world market. It is very important that the Indian entrepreneur as the manager, develops that self-respect which is possible only when he knows who he is, what are his roots, where he comes from. In other words, you must have a very self-rooted worldview. In fact we say that in this country we have the philosophy of "*Vasudhaiva Kutumbakam*" and "*Easavasyam idamsarvam.*" It is the great philosophy that the "Whole universe is one family" and "God pervades the entire universe." We built a culture based on that worldview, but our problem was that we could not defend that culture. President Clinton in his inaugural address said: "I am ready to defend at any cost the American way of life." Can the Indian Prime Minister say that? Will he say from the ramparts of the Red Fort, "I am ready to defend the culture, the way of life of India?" For one thing, there is no way of life at all; there is nothing to defend; we have created nothing valuable of late. Therefore, it is very important that not only should we create a way of life, but also be ready to defend it.

We must have something to defend. So, what is our way of life? What are the roots of our culture? And what governs our policies, our worldview? This is very important and hence we are going into the cultural root of our country. Friends, we have important books—the Upanishads, the *Bhagavad Gita*, the Puranas, the Dharamsastras and various other texts which expound our view and our way of life. Today, we will be discussing only one text, the *Bhagavad Gita*. We will see what it can teach us, the managers and leaders of this country.

We know that the *Gita* was taught on a battlefield. The context of the *Bhagavad Gita* is very important. It was taught to Arjuna on the battlefield, when Arjuna was confronted with one of the greatest crises of his life. Unable to bear the stress and strain he collapsed on the battlefield, on the floor of his chariot, and Bhagavan taught him the *Gita*. Since the context of the *Bhagavad Gita* is the battlefield where people came together to fight it out, the *Gita* teachings are important to the modern manager because we are also fighting in the market place and want to be competitive. As one of the managers told me: "We are like dogs. It is a dog fight, my dear Swamiji. I need my bone I am fighting for it." The second aspect of the *Bhagavad Gita* is that Arjuna was a chief executive, let me put it that way. He was the General commander of the army, and he comes to the battlefield to fight the battle and secure a victory for his forces. But then he collapses, suddenly finding himself lacking in energy. He becomes demotivated, dispirited, fatigued. So, too, when our manager or chief executive faces the challenges and problems of the job, suddenly he finds he has no energy, no enthusiasm, no motivation to fight and eventually collapses. Though he has ideas, he is not able to muster energy to fight on. The *Bhagavad Gita* is important to the modern manager because the problems and the situations he faces are similar to the ones which Arjuna faced. Finally, the teaching takes place to motivate Arjuna, inspire Arjuna, make him fight the battle. At the end of it, after the teaching, Arjuna says: "I have now no doubt at all; all my doubts are dispelled; I am rooted now and am ready to be active in the field." So, Arjuna becomes a dynamic worker at the end of the teaching. To sum up, we find Arjuna collapsing on the battlefield at the beginning of the *Gita*. On being revived (reinventing himself) after the *Gita* teaching, he fights the battle and wins it. This is what we also want: How to get that energy, that enthusiasm, that inspiration so that we can not only fight the battle of life but also win it.

How did Bhagavan Sri Krishna motivate Arjuna? Bhagavan motivated Arjuna not by teaching him a new skill or a new technology, nor by importing technology from outside. He only changed the attitude of Arjuna, the vision of Arjuna, the soul experience of Arjuna. Sri Krishna gave him a new way of experiencing himself, a new understanding about himself. Arjuna thought he had no energy, but Bhagavan said: "Arjuna, you have plenty of energy within you. Don't look outward for your energy, your inspiration. You have to look inward." The first teaching was: "Arjuna, intelligent people never grieve over a challenging situation. If you are an enlightened person, you will never sit down, cry and weep, but will face the situation courageously." So, in a nutshell, the first lesson of the *Gita* is: "An enlightened person, an intelligent person will not grieve over the situation." If you grieve, it will make you impotent and disabled. It makes you blind to the situation. You are not able to invoke the energy within yourself. So Bhagavan tells Arjuna: "Face the situation with a smile." And Bhagavan himself teaches with a smiling face. The secret of invoking your energy from within yourself is to face your challenges or problems with a smiling disposition.

Unfortunately we have forgotten how to smile. With the civilisational growth, the first casualty was our capacity to smile. In our country, whenever we start a new venture, we start with a prayer. We do it so that the mind becomes quiet and when the mind is quiet, the energies are unfolded, intelligence functions, and the brain becomes optimal. But when there is a cloud of emotions covering your intelligence, the brain becomes dull. "Why should I pray?" the so-called intellectual asks. Or you may be a university graduate, so arrogant that prayer and mediation are considered unfashionable. Why don't you meditate? When you meditate, you keep your mind quiet, silent. But silence is not possible because our mind is like a railway station crowded with thoughts coming and going. If we cannot pray or observe silence to begin with, at least let us begin our dialogue or discussion or board meetings with a smile. Let there be a two-minute smiling session. When the chairman starts smiling, the front row people start smiling too and then the whole assembly roars with laughter. When you laugh, your eyes dilate, your nervous system cools down and because of that, the brain functions and then creative decisions can be taken. The first rule of management should be: "Face your problems with a smile."

Some of the motivational techniques used by Lord Krishna, to begin with, did not move Arjuna. Lord Krishna tried to evoke the pride of Arjuna, his self-respect. "Why do you behave like this, in a chicken-hearted way? Arjuna, this is unbecoming of you. This is heaven-denying. This will bring lasting ignominy," the Lord says. This is one way to motivate people, especially North Indians – you invoke their warrior nature, you invoke the heroism in them. You have to motivate people differently because India is a conglomerate of various ethnic and linguistic traditions. This is where a Harvard-educated man fails. He is not able to touch a deep chord in the individual. So, one method of motivating is invoking his pride. It may be national pride, or pride in the company he works for, perhaps pride in his religion.

Arjuna was still not motivated. You may talk about the national glory, or regional glory. When you talk about national glory, you also talk about increasing production and all that, but what does labour get out of it, what do I get out of it? Earlier Arjuna used to get inspired this way – when he was in his 20s just out of the management institute. But do you think you will be able to persuade him like this now that he is a hard-boiled, cynical, greedy person? You can't motivate such a person by invoking national pride. Then Bhagavan says: "All right, Arjuna if you don't fight this battle, if you don't face this challenge, it will bring you ill-fame." Arjuna is known in the world as an effective executive, and various companies are trying to rope him in for his knowledge, stature and experience. Bhagavan, therefore, says: "If you are running away from this battle, Arjuna, that will bring you lasting ill-fame. You have to fight". But Arjuna looks blank and again he collapses. That also does not influence him. "I am tired of my glory. In fact, I know what is my worth. It is all an illusion which people have created," says Arjuna. So, glory also does not inspire him.

Bhagavan continues to talk to him. "It is your duty. You

must fight this battle because it is your duty." Arjuna thinks about it for some time and again he says he is not motivated at all. The call of duty, which we did hold during the independence struggle as our fundamental duty to this country, and we were inspired by it but now even that is not able to inspire us. It is sheer greed which seems to be inspiring us.

Three clarion calls failed – sense of pride, prospect of glory, and duty.

Now, how to inspire Arjuna to fight the battle? Then Bhagavan thought that he had to change the whole attitude of Arjuna – his worldview had to be changed, his vision had to be overhauled. This is where philosophy comes to the rescue otherwise Bhagavan should have talked to Arjuna about the latest technology which is going on in the battlefield and all that. In the entire *Bhagavad Gita* there is no discussion on strategies for war. He discusses the ways and means of changing Arjuna's mind, to shift his consciousness from one focus to another focus.

Again, Bhagavan says to Arjuna: "An intelligent man will never cry over an adverse situation, he will courageously face it." So, the second rule is: "Never run away from a challenge," because the challenge is a handy opportunity to know who you are and what are your energies. I may have penty of energy, but if I don't face the challenge, my energy will not be known to myself. It is very important that we always welcome a challenge. As we interact with the challenge, we are able to invoke our own inner potential. The basic faith of the Indian religion is that the individual is infinitely endowed. Fortunately our attention in modern management practices has shifted from machines and from techniques to the individual and attitudes, to motivating the individual, to discovering his power, to empowering him. This calls for a philosophy and a worldview. How can you empower an individual if he has no power within himself? So, the basic understanding is, "You are infinite power, you are children of immortality – *amritasya putrah*." "*Tattvamasi, Shivoham*," is the *mantra* which we are taught by the rishis to chant whenever we feel depressed. Our rishis say: Withdraw into the puja room where you keep suggesting to yourself, "Shivoham, shivoham." The idea of Shivoham is, 'You are infinite, you have infinite power untapped within yourself. Tap that power.' *Shivoham* means 'I am okay'. If you say that you are okay, then you will be able to face the situation. It is our responsibilty to constantly say to ourselves that we are okay. You don't need a psychiatrist to say that. If you tell yourself that you are okay and you are infinite energy, then you really have it and nobody can deny it to you. If you yourself say that you don't have the energy, who can give you that energy? You have to lift yourself by your own bootstraps ... Don't condemn yourself because if you condemn and belittle yourself, you become your own enemy. So, a manager who says, 'I have no energy (power); the government is responsible for that, my workers are responsible for that, the degraded technology is responsible for the low productivity and so on," is only making excuses.

The quality of the individual is more important, and that is invoked from within oneself. This is the third teaching of the *Bhagavad Gita* – you have to go within yourself and suggest continuously to yourself positive thoughts. Nowadays medical science also says the same thing. When you suggest, "I am okay, I am Shiva", the brain itself produces certain electrical impulses which activate the whole body system. Hanuman in the Ramayana was just as purposeless as an unemployed youth, serving a king without a country. He met Rama and immediately got a vision in life to discover his energy. Hanuman thought that he would not be able to cross the ocean to land in Lanka, but when Jambavan told him, "You have it within you," he discovered it. In the same way it is very important that we suggest to ourselves constantly that we are okay, never suggesting that we have no energy at all.

The next teaching of the *Gita* is the importance of keeping our mind quiet all the time. Not only must you suggest that you have the energy; to invoke that energy the mind has to be kept quiet also. When the mind is quiet, the energy can be invoked. A manager, if he wants to be effective and invoke his new energies and enthusiasm, must keep his mind quiet because all his subordinates, boss and competitors will try to psychologically disturb him. It is the psychology that matters most. It is not a battle in terms of product or quality or anything else. The first battle is won when he psychologically puts the other person down. The opposition will always try to confuse him, belittle him, to put funny ideas to him. Therefore, it is very important that we must not react at all. Our problem is that we react. If somebody calls you a donkey, you start doubting it may be true; then you won't have that certain, undoubted knowledge that "I am not a donkey but a human being." Suppose somebody very powerfully suggests to you, "Sir, you are stupid.' You will sometimes prove it by reacting. Therefore, it is very important that you don't bite the bait that is put before you by the other person.

Non-reaction is an important lesson taught by Bhagavan to Arjuna. "Whatever be the successes or failures, you should not react to the situation." Though you do not react, you should certainly *respond* to the situation. Please understand that. You have to respond to the situation, analyse the situation. Then there should be a correct measure of response, no more, no less. And that requires a fine tuning of the mind which is only possible when the mind is quiet. A word of warning: in success one should not get elated because the next attempt may turn out to be a failure. You should also not get depressed by a failure because, if you become depressed, you will not able to learn what went wrong. The *Bhagavad Gita* says in effect: "Gentlemen, you have a choice over your actions but you have no choice over the fruits of your action."

This advice of the Gita confuses people, especially in the

modern world where everybody asks, "What will I get?" But the *Gita* says: "Don't ask what you will get out of it." One might question whether it is not greed being taught in modern management institutions. When you ask the question, "What will I get out of my toil?" Bhagavan says: "You work with a certain goal in mind, but you may not be able to get the expected goal by your effort." This is a truth. We often do not command an expected result by our effort. The question is, when we fail to get our expected result, how are we going to react? You can react in two ways.

(1) You can say, "I am a useless person. I don't think I will ever achieve it, nobody in our family made it." Thereby, you develop an inferiority complex. You develop an inferiority complex merely because of one failure. One failure makes you a total failure.

(2) But an intelligent person will not react that way. "It is only one failure, I am not a total failure. I am not useless, but only that my energies have been used less." Thus when you are not reacting negatively to a situation, you are able to learn what went wrong and you can improve upon your performance. What Bhagavan says is a very scientific law. Recently, a delegation went to America and they were invited to the White House. In the President's office they saw an inscription which read: "You can become a better performing manager or an executive if you don't bother who gets the rewards for your work." Or, in other words, "If I can work without expecting a reward, then I can perform

138

better." When the Americans say so, you accept it, but when the *Gita* says the same thing you hesitate to accept it, which shows a kind of mental slavery. The *Gita* says, "Don't react," because reaction steadily reduces your energy.

The first teaching was: Accept that we have plenty of energy which has to be invoked. The second, that it can be invoked when you don't run away from a situation, and the third, to invoke it, you must keep your mind quiet all the time. Neither react to success nor to failure. Only respond to situations. This is the crux of the teaching of Bhagavan.

Arjuna was taught to self-motivate. There is no other technique of motivation discussed in the *Gita*. Therefore, motivation is to change your attitude to your life, your goals. Arjuna discovers a new, a higher, goal. All this time Arjuna's goal was money, power and indulgence. He had enjoyed these fully; in fact he had even been to Swargaloka – Swargaloka means modern America. He got money, name (*Dhananjaya* means very rich *Parantapa*, a competitor). A person who has money, power and facilities to enjoy, cannot be motivated that way. So Bhagavan awakened him to a new goal called *Shreyas*. *Shreyas* means "the total, spiritual, holistic satisfaction", which comes when you work without expectation. It comes from an opportunity where you can discover yourself, invoke yourself. Even the Maslovain hierarchy of values admits self-actualisaton as the highest value. What is self-actualisation? It is freedom to do whatever you want to do; a situation where you have the freedom to freely unfold, to be yourself. If I want to clean *chappals* in a temple, I must have the inner freedom to do that. You and I don't have that freedom. Your self-respect depends upon others, on their opinions and values. Hence, a really free person, a person who can actualise himself, must have the freedom to be whatever he is. That is the true freedom. That should be the ultimate goal of a manager.

However, usually we are conditioned by stereotyped role expectations. A particular dress is given and you have to behave in a particular way. The moment he wears that dress, he starts to change. For example, take the police officer. Once he slips into that uniform he is a different person. Here, the uniform conditions your response. A true executive is one whose behaviour and responses are not conditioned by a particular role; he has the freedom to take any role, leave that role and move further. This is known as 'transcendental leadership'. There you become a true *sanyasi*. A true *sanyasi* has the freedom to be whatever he is and, therefore, his responses are not conditioned by situations but spring from his original creativity. If you want to create a creative atmosphere in the country, we must have such transcendental *sanyasi* type leaders. So, Bhagavan gave a new goal to Arjuna, a new discovery: "Work has to become a means of discovering yourself." Work is not just to produce something. The aim of work is that in the process I am bringing out a piece of my soul in it. The soul is infinite.

Infinite ideas can come out of it. So, Bhagavan says to Arjuna: "In this state of consciousness what you do will not define you. In fact you will define your work situation and the work situation will not affect you at all." That is the goal Arjuna was given, which really inspired him. Arjuna says: "I have become the master of my destiny. What I do has nothing to do with me. I will give respect to my work, not that work will give me respect." That kind of awareness arises in Arjuna. Bhagavan gives Arjuna a new goal, a new way of looking at life. It transforms Arjuna's personality, and he discovers new energy and plunges into activity.

Churning as a Yajna Culture

Arjuna's changed attitude can be seen as a new work culture. The *Bhagavad Gita* talks about the *yajna* culture. A cosmic example of the *yajna* culture is the "Churning of the milky ocean". The churning of the ocean was an attempt to reinvent a society, to recreate a society. Let me give you a background of this story.

The *devas* (gods) became old and did not have the energy to do anything. They had become a senile society, an obsolete society with no more creativity in them. Everybody was thinking about old things and they were afraid of everybody. So they went to Lord Vishnu, the protector of all. Vishnu is the perfect manager. He relaxes all the time on a couch called *ananta* (bliss). He gets work done through others. Seven rishis sit around and invoke his glories. Whenever he feels low, the rishis render the *Vishnusahasranama* with Vishnu quietly lying down. Don't think he is not aware of things. He is actually in *yoga nidra* where the mind is absolutely calm but very alert. He is lying down, but life continues and he does not interfere in anything. The mere awareness is sufficient to bring order to a society. Vishnu never interferes.

Let us see what happens here. Everywhere the manager or the chief executive interferes and therefore nothing happens. Are we not seeing it in our homes? Children do not study, they play and fight instead. The mother shouts and orders them to study but the children do not listen. Then the mother takes a broomstick and hits them which causes the children to cry (the mother also cries). Ultimately the mother asks them to go to sleep (they need not study). The whole thing began because the mother wanted the child to study and, finally, there is no study because the mother interfered. She descends to the level of the child and loses the authority to control. Whereas how does the father control? He is sitting upstairs reading a newspaper while the children are playing and fighting. The mother has only to say, "Daddy is upstairs." Daddy will hear this, but will not come down. He will only clear his throat to announce his presence and that is sufficient to calm the children. To control, it is sufficient to make your presence felt. You need to be alert and aware.

So, Vishnu tells the *devas*: "Do one thing; churn the milky ocean." I tell you this story because it is such an inexhaustible reservoir of ideas. But because of our stupidity, arrogance and ignorance, we ignore our rich heritage and what we can learn from it.

When Vishnu says "Churn the milky ocean" what does he mean? Milk is white and stands for the mind. The mind is also made of *sattva*. So, milky ocean means the collective potential, the collective unconscious where ideas are embedded. All ideas which come into the society, come into the individual, are all embedded in our unconsciousness. Vishnu then told the *devas*: "You alone cannot churn it, you need a churning rod. Go to Manthara, the mountain and ask for one. And the churning rope should be even more powerful. Go to Vasuki, the king of snakes. Two sets of people are necessary to churn it, to draw the churning rod back and forth. Seek the help of all including your enemies, the *asuras*." It is a great lesson for the modern manager. Don't say, "He is my enemy, he is a useless person, he is a trade union leader, etc." Whenever we want to undertake a national activity, a creative activity, we have to take the help of all people. We have to enlist the support of all in society. Nobody should be excluded from our national reconstruction work.

Then Vishnu cautioned the *devas* of one thing: "When the churning goes on, Vasuki, since he is a snake, will vomit poison. Therefore somehow make sure that you don't stand on the head side of Vasuki, or else the poison will kill all the topmost managers." How to achieve that, how to make the *asuras* accept that we are *devas*, the superior ones, and therefore should stand on the head side of Vasuki even when that is not where we really want to be. The *asuras* will say: "No! No. How do you say that? If you want our support … What do you think of us, etc." You should pretend not to agree. You should say that the tail is the inferior side and you want the superior side. Then after a lot of argument and hesitation, finally you must grudgingly accept the tail side and make the *asuras* feel that you are giving them a concession. This is the art of negotiation and we can say the negotiations went off successfully. The *asuras* were happy that they had won a point. It was now their prestige issue, that the churning must go on because the *devas* had conceded them a point. For success you have to make the other person also see the winning situation. "It is not only my victory, but yours too." You put the right person at the right place by this kind of manoeuvre.

The churning goes on and things start appearing. Let us not think of Indian culture as "other-worldly". That is the biggest illusion we hold. Indian culture is a harmonious blend of material progress and spiritual well-being which we called *shreyas*. At the end of the *Bhagavad Gita* it is said, "Victory, success, well-being are all necessary" (XVII - 78). So, during the churning, first Lakshmi (wealth) came; a lot of wealth was created. Then came the *Kamdhenu* (cow), then *Kalptaru* and then the poison. Before the emergence of poison, Manthara started slipping (going down), indicating that the morale of the people is sinking. It happens. Often we are not able to sustain our enthusiasm all the time. Sometimes our will sags. The people involved in the productive activity become dispirited. As Manthara starts slipping, Vishnu comes down in the form of a tortoise to lift the mountain on his back. So should our top man, the manager or Chief Executive, loosen his tie, roll up his sleeves and come down. Lord Vishnu, though he is quietly lying down all the time, comes down from the ivory tower when something goes radically wrong.

The churning went on and Vasuki vomited poison. Lots of the *asuras* were destroyed but the top people were not affected. Let us think of American society preparing for nuclear war. In the event of a nuclear war, they have an underground system where top leaders will be protected. To preserve any society this kind of preparation is necessary. In the same way, the poison is going to come anyway. In material life, there will be war and it is our duty to preserve the cream of our society. So, a lot of *asuras* were destroyed but not the *devas*. Ultimately comes *amruth* – the final product. Now, who can lay claim to that, or under whose custody should it be kept, is the question. The *asuras* take away the *amruth*. Again Vishnu has to come down, devise a technique, take the *amruth* back and restore it to the *devas* to be kept under their care and control. It means that not only should you create wealth, but it should be kept in the care of good and noble people, people who have the nobility to use it for the welfare of all. In Russia, they nationalised everything, but the means of producton came under the control of crooks. That is why the society collapsed after 70 years.

The story of the churning of the milky ocean indicates the *yajna* spirit. Everybody must come together in work and whatever is produced must be shared, but the wealth should be in the care of good and noble people. This is the kind a *yajna* spirit described in the *Gita* which has a lot of lessons for our work culture. Now, the leadership, the manager, should not blame the followers according to the *Bhagavad Gita* (III - 21). The blame should rest squarely on the leader. If something goes wrong in a factory or university or in the country, the blame must be accepted by the leaders. What the leaders follow, that alone the followers take up. If the standard of your company is going down, the responsibility will rest squarely on the manager, the Chief Executive. So, if you want to revive this country, rejuvenate this country where will we start from? The general theory is that it is *Kaliyuga*, everybody will be like that and so I ought to be like that. This cannot be the statement of a leader. The leader must lead. It is our duty as leaders – and all of you are leaders in your own respective spheres – not to blame the followers. First of all, each one of us must become a point of excellence and then we have to bridge two points of excellences; only then we can create a continent of excellence in this country. But somewhere somebody should start, and who can that somebody be? He should be like Shiva. Shiva swallows the poison but still does not get poisoned. In the same way the leader should take the responsibility; he must take all the problems upon himself and should not feel strained under these responsibilities. Hence Bhagavan says: "The leader is responsible for the problem."

Mahatma Gandhi could galvanise our nation. If one Gandhi could do that, we also can. Sri Rama never complained about the monkeys – "What will I do with them?" – especially when he was to fight a battle. Hanuman was an unemployed person sitting in *Rishyamookachala*, not doing anything. He did not know his power. Once he met with Lord Rama, he became a totally different person. So, let us not complain about our workforce if we are the devotees of Rama who could create a big army and successfully fight a battle with the help of the monkeys. Why can't we then? I should say that the blame for the present state of affairs squarely rests upon you people because you are leaders. Let us not blame the masses. They are ready to do anything for us. Devotion exists in this country. If they are told, "Jump into the well," they will do that, but there is nobody who has the guts to say that. Why have we no guts? It is because we don't know what our goals are. We have not defined our national goal and unless it is done, it is not possible to inspire people.

The *Gita* has many lessons which I may not have the time to expand on now. Most importantly the *Gita* defines our goals. What should be our goal? The modern civilisation is in a crisis now. We have created unprecedented growth with the help of science and technology, but at what cost? The invisible cost of modern economic development, with the ecological problem on one side (we all know that), and the individual cost – the peace of mind, the harmony in the family, etc., on the other. Your heart and health is the ultimate cost.

The *Bhagavad Gita* says, "The more challenges you face, the more integrated you become, the more healthy you become, the more divine you become." Whereas what we see is that the more we work, and the more we go up in the hierarchy, the more sick we become. Almost all Chief Executives are sick people who suffer from diabetes or stomach ulcers. These diseases have become status symbols. We have conquered the ordinary diseases, the traditional ones, but now we are suffering from civilisational diseases. Except the brain every other organ is affected. The brain is unaffected because it is rarely used. If there is no healthy life then how can you lead an organisation? So there is the invisible cost at the personal level and at the environmental level, and yet you say, "I have created wealth." But actually we are like silkworms. The silkworm creates silk around it, surrounding it with a velvety covering, and ultimately the sericulturist comes, puts the worm in hot water, takes the silk out and the worm dies. What a pitiable state! In the whole development, the casualties and disposables are the individuals and yet we talk about individual freedom and individual glory! What have we done? What have we created?

We have built the Pyramids, the great wall of China, the Taj Mahal, but what about the individual? Where is he? Why should he become a casualty? We must have a new strategy for development where the individual is at the centre of our collective concerns. Ultimately the individual must be happy. We must redefine economic goals on a human scale. I think only India can do this. It is only we who have a vision and strategy for it.

I suggest that in the new strategy for development – world development and economic progress – we must have this idea that the ultimate success of an economy or an enterprise lies in the health and wholesome happiness of the individuals constituting that society. If the individual is not happy, that economy is a failure. Take the example of the American economy. They created unprecedented growth but everybody is crazy and sick. They say that when an individual is mad you put him in an asylum; but when a nation becomes crazy, you put it in the Security Council.

The future is beckoning. It is our responsibility to sit down and think seriously instead of simply following other people. And we have the tradition, we have the culture, we have the past. So, let us sit together and take stock of things. Let us exploit the roots of our philosophy and culture so that we can lead the future world. The future is beckoning, and you, as the leaders of a great culture, have to respond to it creatively.

Understanding Mind And Relationship for Individual and Organisational Effectiveness

We are meeting here not only to learn about the mind and relationships, but also to understand what is going on around us, to make sense of the chaotic happenings which are beyond our control. We have to understand mind and relationship in the context of what is happening in this world, not only in our country, in our organisation, in our family and in our own body system. Mind cannot be understood in isolation because mind is a dynamic entity and it comes into life only in relationships. When there is no relationship, when there is no activity, there is no mind. When you are meditating there is no mind. Mind comes when I interact with you, with my neighbours, when I do something,

Lecture under the auspices of Ahmedabad Management Association.

when I have to produce results. It is in action that mind comes into manifestation. Therefore, relationship is very important for the experience of mind. We will, therefore, try to understand mind in terms of productive activities, and also the problems and possibilities of mind.

We undertake all these studies in the context of the liberalisation of the economy because there is incredible traffic in terms of ideas, products, capital and people. Walls of all sorts are coming down – nationalistic, ideological, religious, etc. As the Upanishads say: "Let noble thoughts come from all sides." In that interaction we are benefited, as also others, and in the process we create wealth. So ideologically this liberalisation process is to be welcomed. It brings a fresh breeze from outside. It gives us enough room to grow and to become *Visvamanava* – the Universal person. Unless you grow universally you will not unleash your full potential. Even the full growth of the individual requires a world context. There is no need to panic or to be annoyed about the globalisation process. It is a challenge as well as a problem; and every challenge will have its own set of problems. We have to accept this challenge. We have to think globally and act locally. We have to act keeping this scenario in mind. Let us welcome the globalisation process. Let us prepare ourselves for the 21st century to become world leaders, to contribute our mite, our share, to the global progress. It is in this context that we have assembled here – as leaders of industry, of the corporate world, and to understand our strengths and weaknesses as a country, as a culture, and as individuals.

The organisation has a culture. The individual has a mind. When you say "I", you mean your mind. As an individual it is the mind which defines and distinguishes you from another person besides, of course, the physical differences which do not matter much. Mind is a tool. As the mind, so the person. The world is highly competitive; there is no room for compassion or mercy. We must, therefore, make ourselves fit physically, mentally, spiritually and culturally. Unless we do that we will not be able to participate in this competitive, interactive, evolutionary process that is taking place in the world. The battle is not in militaristic, religious or ideological terms, but is essentially economic. Everybody tries to dominate the world by their productive power. Productivity of the individual, competitiveness of the nation – all these matter. If you are afraid of neo-colonialism the best way to combat it is to become interactive and strong. Even to develop your muscles you have to interact with a stronger person. Unless somebody pushes you into water you will not learn to swim. Initially you hesitate, but once in the water you enjoy the experience. So if you want to survive, you have to be competitive. Competition is not dominance, competition is give-and-take. Let us not be afraid of one country, religion or ideology dominating the world.

Competition also means making your contribution, taking something and in exchange creating a common wealth. Multicultural values are created as transnationals source their activities in different countries and cultures. At the same time we cannot rule out nationalistic and corporate wars for market share at a certain level. India has to be strong. If not there is danger of our resources being sucked away. In this interactive world power centres emerge and unless we can interact from a position of strength we will be exploited and made into an appendage of some big power. We will not be able to participate in "win-win" situations. Remember the bear and hunter story? The hunter was hunting in the jungle and sighted a bear. The hunter wanted a fur coat, and the bear was hungry. The bear convinced the hunter of the complementarity of their needs. In the interaction that followed, the bear appeased its hunger and the hunter got the fur coat. The point is that unless we are strong we cannot beneficially interact, contribute, and create wealth.

These are some of the points we have to think about very closely. We must discover our roots. We must redefine our culture. We must upgrade the productivity of our work force. The starting point is self-respect. A "we can" mindset is to be created. "I can", "we can", "the company can", "the country can" attitude is the first stirring of self-respect. However, this should not be a mere show of arrogance and stubbornness. Self-respect should be based on a clear understanding of our strengths and weaknesses as otherwise we will launch activities without a measure of our strength. The *Bhagavad Gita* calls such initiatives *tamasic*. Hence we must know our culture; we must develop strength and self-respect (*swabhiman*). You may be Westernised, but you will still be conditioned by your culture and initial upbringing. So the knowledge of one's culture and tradition is a part of self-knowing and self-respect. In addition we must also have the freedom and creative intelligence to interact with other cultures, traditions and peoples.

We have words like *brahma, maya, dharma, karma, yajna* which define our worldview. These are much misunderstood words. Suppose you don't want to pay for somebody's work, or honour a contract, you hide behind a faulty interpretation of *maya* or *karma* – "All this is *maya;*" "it is your *karma;*" "*sab Bhagavan ki iccha hai,*" etc. How to interpret, understand and apply these common words in daily life is very important.

Ours is a holistic worldview. We look upon the whole world as a living organism rather than a machine. The Western scientific worldview is mechanist: as an assemblage of nuts and bolts, which can be assembled, dismantled, measured and modified at will. But how can you do that to human beings and to nature? An organism is a living, dynamic entity which is more than its constituent parts whereas a machine is just the sum total of its parts. Do you look at the world and human beings as mere machines or as organisms with a life force which we call variously as soul, *atman*, the god principle or the heart? Increasingly modern science is veering round to such a holistic worldview. We have to build an economic perspective, a value system and a culture based on this worldview. It is against this background that we will analyse mind and relationship for individual efficiency and organisational effectiveness.

It is not out of context that I raised the above issues. You are managers and you want to create wealth. As managers you do not expect to hear about the esoteric concept of *moksha* from me. But, in fact, I am going to talk about the creation of wealth and how wealth-creating activities are related to the ultimate human goal of *moksha*. We are going to see how wealth creation itself can become an extremely fulfilling spiritual experience. *Moksha*, or living in God consciousness, is not opposed to the creation of wealth. You can create wealth as a *sadhana*. What is *sadhana*? It is a way of doing your work; that work itself becomes a means of invoking your divinity within. Creation of wealth, or any other such productive activities, can help you to develop a mature mind, a deep mind. Wealth-creating activities can thus become a way of exploring your inner potential. We see no difference between material and spiritual life. *Kathopanishad* says (IV-10): "Whatever is here that alone is there. Whoever says God is there, and the world is different from God, will go from death to death." Therefore, one has to see the complementarity of world and God, of body and soul. This is the holistic approach and our tradition is rooted in it. Why should we not understand it and organise our economic activities accordingly?

Moksha is the highest *purushartha* (goal). You are engaged in making money (*Artha*). Unfortunately in our country anybody who creates wealth is suspected of being corrupt. He is taken to be an immoral exploiter. This attitude should change. You must feel proud as creators of wealth. In the *sastra* it is said that *Dharma* and *Kama* are based on *Artha* – "*Artha mulau dharma kamau*." Please learn this saying in Sanskrit so that you can think in perspective, and you have the right vocabulary. Our main problem is not lack of right thoughts but the absence of right vocabulary. We are weak in communication. We know that wealth is very important, but we cannot support that understanding with a logically acceptable proposition. So remember these words from *Panchatantra*: "Comforts and goodness (*Kama and Dharma*) depend on wealth (*Artha*)." If you have wealth you can lead an honest and happy life. Let there be no doubt that *Artha* is very important. Let us clear another common misperception by remembering another wise saying: "Body is the primary instrument of living a good life" (*Sareeram adyam khalu dharma sadhanam*).

Before going into what is the mind, let me explain a few more concepts. We have used the words mind, relationship, individual and organisation. Mind is an individual phenomenon; it is the focal point of creativity. When individuals come together, organisation comes into existence. The capacity of individuals to form an organisation is very important because no productive activity can be undertaken without an organisation. An organisation needs trust. People must trust each other to form an organisation, to identify an area of operation, to carry out the operation and produce results. Efficiency is the quality of the individual depending upon his skill, knowledge and attitude. But effectiveness is an organisational property. What is effectiveness? It is people coming together setting aside their immediate comforts and considerations to form groups and achieve results. In simple terms, effectiveness is the capacity to deliver in a given situation. There are efficient people who can individually produce results but in a group they cannot because of vanity, arrogance, a superiority complex, contempt for others, impatience, etc. They have intellectual ability but lack emotional stability. They have an IQ, but no EQ. An IQ can get you a job, but EQ (emotional intelligence) alone can take you to the top. University rank holders become colossal failures in teaching work; in an organisation they become misfits because they don't have enough EQ, or soft skills. Emotional quotient is a function of values and attitudes, a right side brain function. In our culture we call it *ida*. The left side brain function is called *pingala*. That is why people who lack emotional stability gain it by breathing through the right nostril. There is a definite correlation between mind and effectiveness. Most of one's emotions manifest with relation to other individuals. IQ can be developed by reading books or listening to talks. By yourself, you can develop intelligence, or memory power, but when you come into association with other people you find yourself wanting.

What you are looking for is individual efficiency and organisational effectiveness which finally boils down to the mind of the individual. If you understand the mind, you can manage any situation. Modern management is also concerned with the individual. The focus is on HRD, rather than on technology, capital or resources for that matter. It is the people behind machines that matter. What is important is not technology or raw materials but ideas which add value to the product. And where do ideas come from? Not from books but from the mind. You have to sit quiet if you want access to that 'quantum soup' within you where things are processed and recreated in infinite ways. Unless you touch that level you cannot be creative. Hence, to invoke ideas, which contribute 90 per cent of the value of the product, mind is extremely important.

Secondly, since managers deal with people they have to inspire them to work. Those who deal with people are managers, and those who deal wih managers become leaders. One who just deals with a machine is a mechanic. A mechanic need not be good with people. Conversely, a manager may not be comfortable with machines. An entrepreneur is one who encompasses all these three functions. We need entrepreneurs in this country who can take risks, who can envision, who can put heart and soul into their efforts. Once an idea takes hold of them, they won't sleep until they transform that idea into reality, into a product. They are like Arjuna, the great *Mahabharata* hero, who never sleeps (*gudakesa*) till a new skill is mastered. Arjuna is also called Dhananjaya – winner of wealth. Another epithet of Arjuna is *Paramtapa* – Terror of his enemies. These are the same qualities expected of a modern entrepreneur.

When you deal with another mind, you have to inspire it to work. A mechanic does not need to inspire a machine. Even if he abuses the machine it still works! On the other hand, if you abuse a person he will balk. Why? Because you are dealing with his mind, with his spirit. Unless you learn to respect him you will not be able to bring out the best in him.

How to study the mind? You cannot observe the mind in a test tube, or under the microscope. The mind cannot be objectified. Therefore studying the mind means to study one's own mind. If you know how your mind functions, then you also understand all the lanes and bylanes, the entire labyrinthian criss-crossing, of any mind.

I will present the Indian view of the mind's function. Mind is the tool of work, and comes into operation in interaction. Mind has to be understood in its dynamic interplay. You cannot stop the mind to study it. Innumerable factors influence the mind at any given moment, factors that are known, unknown, quantifiable, nonquantifiable etc., and which never manifest except for their effect. Such is the complexity of mind.

Understanding one's mind is the key to understanding all minds. Hence the ancient dictum: "Know thyself."

The Western thinkers conceived mind differently. Rene Descartes said that mind is different from matter, that matter can be studied independent of mind. It helped the development of scientific thinking and objective study of the world. Now this theory is being disputed and the mind-matter connection is being studied.

Modern physical science has dispensed with matter. It has travelled a long way from molecules, to atoms, protons, neutrons, electrons, measons to quantum collapse and the uncertainty principle. Finally physicists say that matter is nothing but energy. Whether energy is particle or wave is still not known. They say that it is the observer's choice to experience matter as particle or wave – meaning it involves consciousness which is a vital datum in experience. Therefore, ultimately, matter is not even energy, because the energy function depends on the observer. Finally, what is there? Consciousness. There is only *chaitanya* and nothing else. Everything else is only a manifestation of that consciousness; it is the dance of Shiva, *Shiva thandavam*. Our rishis had come to this understanding long, long ago. Ultimately intelligence is the ground reality. In Vedanta this ground of everything is known as *brahman*. Today the terminology is different and we talk about the quantum soup which is the source of all manifestations.

If you can access the quantum soup, or *brahman*, and let thoughts spring from that, you can fulfill all those thoughts. This is the field of all potentialities. You can as well call it quantum soup, or *chaitanya*, Shiva, *brahman*, or the basket of all possibilities. A thought emerging from this awareness will be most creative; hence intention backed by attention makes for natural, effortless materialisation. If you give attention to your infinite potential (invoking infinite energy in you) and then intend a desire (giving direction to the attention-energy) that desire shall be fulfilled. The only caveat is that you must be deeply rooted.

It is a law: attention-intention-materialisation. But our thoughts are not that deep. That is why we produce weak organisations, weak products and hollow services. We have seen that matter finally resolves into consciousness. The Hindu concepts of Shiva and Shakti (as Consciousness and Energy) therefore correspond to modern thinking. The entire world is a manifestation of interaction between Shiva and Shakti. The mind-matter duality dissolves into an all encompassing Consciousness. If only our leaders were to be alive to these wonderful ideas they could create a new India.

Theories about the mind

Another point of debate is regarding the location of the mind. Where is the mind situated? Plato believed that the mind is located in the head (brain). The spherical perfection of the cranium led Plato to house a perfect mind there. Aristotle believed that the mind is seated in the heart. Others say that mind is in the navel region. Deep feelings and thoughts cause a stir in the area around the navel. When you are agonising over something don't you feel butterflies in the stomach? Meditation takes into account all the three regions – the head, the heart and the navel. There is head lotus meditation, heart lotus meditation, and navel lotus meditation.

In the modern age, Dr. Sigmund Freud is considered as the father of the study of the mind. According to him the mind is nothing but an expression of your suppressions and repressions. Mind has two dimensions – the conscious and the unconscious; 10 per cent is conscious and 90 per cent is unconscious. The unconscious mind is your suppressions and repressions while the conscious mind is the expression of those suppressions and repressions. He believed that mind is an energy called the "eros". In our *Agamasastra* the corresponding term is *kundalini*, which lies in two-and-a-half coils at the root of the spinal column causing the three basic passions of lust, anger and greed – to procreate, to protect and to perpetuate. All your basic energies are used up in protecting yourself, in aggression and in hoarding. These passions define you. Suppose you suddenly spot a king cobra in this room, I am sure you will forget all your dignity, who you are, where you are, etc., and run for the door knocking down everybody on the way. Once you reach safety you stop and start behaving like a gentleman again. Why? Your basic existence was threatened. Under pressure, people regress to their real selves, that composed of aggression, anger, and fear. The other selves are mere pretentions. You preserve yourselves by eating food. With regard to this you become greedy and possessive. Producing children is a basic level activity of lust. *Kundalini* is the energy governing all these basic passions. According to Freud too, "eros" governs our conscious and unconscious activities. At the conscious level of the mind exist civilisation, discipline, hypocrisy. But conscious activities are controlled, governed and determined by our unconscious drives and urges. Your liking for somebody is not always rational. All the reasons that you give – like he is intelligent, hard working etc., – are underpinned by reasons unknown to yourself. Your unconscious is at work.

According to the Adlerain theory mind comes into manifestation in the effort to dominate and control. Everybody wants to either dominate or be dominated, rule or be ruled, teach or be taught, love or be loved. Either you are on the side of the suppressor or on the side of the suppressed. The mind see-saws between the desire to dominate and the desire to be dominated. That is the logic of power.

Then came the Marxian theory. It said that the mind is nothing but a reflection of material relationships. There are productive relationships in the society. According to the Marxian conception mind is only an epiphenomenon of a productive, material and historical relationship. The mind is powerless; matter is powerful. However, modern psychologists say that mind dominates matter. All these ideas are partly true, and partly false. The truth is actually hidden somewhere in the din of the clash of these ideas. All of them have a grain of truth, but not Truth *per se*.

The Vedic View

Let us now see how our *sastras* look at the phenomenon of mind. Mind (or *antahkarana*) has four functions: *chitta*, *ahamkara*, *mana* and *buddhi*.

1. **Chitta** is the storehouse of memory, of impressions gathered from past experiences similar to the Freudian unconscious.

2. **Ahamkara**, ego, is a function of memory, the one who relates to experiences and knows "I am the experiencer".

The ego and memory reinforce each other. They are interactive. Your memory is conditioned by ego, your self-image. According to your self-image you gather memories. If you have a poor self-image, you gather those memories which are comfortable for you. When a person who has been called an idiot right from his childhood suddenly hears a word of praise, his face lights up. That word of appreciation creates a powerful memory in him. Similarly, a person who has been called brilliant, but after joining a company comes to be called 'stupid' by his boss, gets deeply hurt, and that experience becomes a powerful memory in him. His self-image conditions his memory, and his memory conditions his self-image. It is a dynamic, ongoing process.

The *ahamkara* or ego says: "I did", "I said", etc. This *ahamkara* keeps on relating to work and its results as "mine". He ignores the contribution of others, but focuses and identifies with his own contribution. This state is known as ignorance (*ajnana*), which means ignoring the whole and seeing only a part. You see only a tree, but not the whole forest. The whole city is stinking, but your house is clean and you are content with that. That is ignorance. You have made phenomenal wealth, but your health suffers. Your neighbourhood is neglected, your family is ignored, but still you say you are successful. That is ignorance. You say that you have a well-cultivated intellect, you are well-informed and up-to-date, but what about your emotions? Can you share your bounty with others? Can you enjoy playing with your grandchildren? Do you have the time, attitude and leisure? Can you just watch the sunrise and stand there mesmerised even as you hurry to the office? If you cannot do all that, that is ignorance. It is because you concentrate only on a part of your life.

3. **Mana** is the seat of passions, feelings, emotions and instincts.

4. **Buddhi** is the faculty of reason, discernment, and decision-making.

There are various permutations and combinations of the

above faculties resulting in different modifications. *Mana* and *chitta* can create powerful imaginations, the result of a mix of passion and past experiences. You may imagine that A is your enemy whereas he may be actually your good friend. Your imagination can be negative or positive and sometimes it can take one to the heights. But no imagination is possible without some basic experience.

Buddhi and *ahamkara* can create stubbornness and fundamentalistic dispositions since you are convinced of your infallibility. You don't progress, because you are stuck with a little knowledge which is euphemistically called specialisation. That is tunnel vision which actually is no vision. You see only that which you want to see and miss the whole picture. It is known as organised ignorance. Such a scholar talks on and on, but does not touch the core; there is no spark of wisdom in his words, only avoidable heat. Specialisation is knowing more and more about less and less. Ultimately you know everything about nothing. It is known as academic blindness. We must be careful about all these so that we remain humble and open. The quality of an intelligent person is his humility, openness, transparency and sensitivity.

The working of the mind (*antahkarana*) is strongly influenced by likes and dislikes. Here calculation and habit play vital roles. Suppose you calculate that such and such a person can harm you, then you develop a dislike for him. Or if a person hurt you in the past you nurse a dislike for him.

The entire operation of the mind is coloured by likes and dislikes.

Ego (*ahamkara*) is a function of the mind. We are not making any value judgement about ego. We can decide later whether ego is good or bad. Let us first understand the mechanism of the mind. Initially ego helps your growth but later it becomes a hindrance. It is like the pole in polevault. You run with a pole (ego), dig it and heave yourself with its help and as you cross the bar the pole is left behind. Some people forget to leave the pole and lose the game. Our problem is that of not knowing when to use the ego and when to drop it. Also if you fail to make it in the first try, come back, pick up the pole (ego) again and try a second time. Therefore, don't destroy the ego, but only use it sparingly and profitably. Ego gives you certain point of reference, a certain point of view, but you must know its limitations and possibilities. Ego has a certain role to play, and after that is done put ego in its place. Command the ego, make him work and then dismiss him. But that power over the ego will come to you only when you come to know That which is beyond the ego, beyond the mind.

The whole *antahkarana* – ego, passions, memory, *buddhi* which constitute the mind – is coloured by likes and dislikes which originate from various sweet and bitter experiences. In analysing the dynamics of the mind we are searching for a set of tools to enable us to handle and operate the mind as we interact with the world. If you don't have that grip over the mind you may become a philosopher but definitely not a man of action. Here we are talking to managers who are men of action.

Though likes and dislikes have their origin in *chitta* and *ahamkara*, at any given moment they have an existence of their own influencing *chitta* and *ahamkara*. It is something like a person you have recruited who becomes part of your organisation, eventually influencing and contributing to the dynamics of the organisation. In the same way likes and dislikes influence your personality.

The following propositions are helpful in the understanding of the dynamics of mind:

(i) You are what you think you are. If you think that you are a useless person, you become useless. In Vedanta we say, if you think you are Shiva, you are Shiva; if you think you are *shava*, you are *shava* (corpse).

(ii) You become what you want to become; thought by thought you can recreate yourself.

(iii) You are responsible for your happiness and unhappiness. It is the way you choose to respond to a situation which makes you happy or unhappy. Happiness or unhappiness is a matter of self-perception, and does not depend upon the situation. It is like seeing the empty half of the glass, while others will see it as half full. The optimist seeing the roses and the pessimist the thorns.

GUNA ANALYSIS OF PERSONALITY

RULING GUNA	CHARACTERISTICS						
	Works	Commitment	Care	Memory	Passion	Reason	Product age & Energy
SATTVA	Steady & Leisurely	To Organisation goals, Shared values & Higher Purposes	Sensitive to others' needs & Understands feelings	Of Both sides of events & Balanced	For Altruistic Ideals To do good To be good	Subtle Discerning & Harmonious	42-56 years Intellec
RAJAS	Spasmodic & Workaholic	To Ego Name Fame & Power	Honour Protective to subordinates	One sided Remembers only what is convenient	To fight To argue To prove a point	Sharp Quick Aggressive & Divisive	26-42 years Passion
TAMAS	Lazy indifferent & Procastinate	To Bad Habits Rumours & Sleep	Slavish or Impudent Easily Swayed	Hazy cannot recall right things at the right time	Mulish & Suicidal	Faulty & Stubborn	14-28 years Physic
GUNATITA	Effortless Spontaneous & Inspiring	Transparent Univolved & Complete	Compassion-ate Giving Sharing Non-possessive	Techno-logical without Psycho-logical baggage	All encom-passing & Motiveless	Nth dimen-sional & All-seeing	Timele Ageless

Figure 1

(iv) Memory dominates the entire field of the mind. Memory can be divided into psychological and technological. Technological memory is what you have learnt practically about the world – your medical, engineering and mathematical knowledge; whatever has been stored in the left side of the brain. Along with the gathering of technological memory, which makes you a competent person, you also gather psychological memories. You still remember the professor who taught you physics, the one who favoured another boy in the class and how you hated him. The memories which you carry in your memory bank – of hatefulness, dislikes, jealousies and all that – are known as psychological memory. What disturbs your mind is psychological memory. The recalling of technological memory is impeded by psychological memory. A face you like, you immediately remember; a face you intensely dislike also you remember. But their impact on the efficiency of the mind are different. You find it hard to remember the face of a person towards whom you are indifferent. Both the memories become jumbled up as you recall technological memory. The psychological dust kicked up covers the former, paints it, varnishes it, with the result that your mind is disturbed and vision clouded. There should be a sieving system in the mind so that psychological memory is sifted out as you recall technological memory which is very important for practical life. You notice this mixing up in meditation. When you try to concentrate on something, dissimilar thoughts disturb you; your anxieties and worries, which are part of psychological memory, interfere at unexpected moments to disturb your whole system.

(v) Mind and its functions can be graded according to the preponderance of *gunas* in its make-up (Refer Figure1). The *gunas* are *satva*, *rajas* and *tamas* – (SRT). Accordingly persons can be classified as *satvic*, *rajasic* and *tamasic* – the contemplative, the active and the passive respectively. The *gunas* influence your psychological and technological memories, ego, likes and dislikes, reasoning (*buddhi*), thinking (*chitta*) and passions (*mana*).

Apart from these three (SRT), there is one more type – the *Gunatita* – the one who is beyond the play of *gunas*. The person who can handle the *gunas* in a detached manner, is the person rooted in his Self. It has to be mentioned in this context that no individual is made up of one *guna* exclusively. There is constant interplay between the basic tendencies (SRT), the conditioning from past memories and desires (known as *vasanas*), and because of the interplay it becomes possible to effect changes in thinking, and so in behaviour.

Let us understand how the mind comes to life (See Figure 2). You know the world through the mind. The information comes through five channels – eye (form), ears (sound), skin (touch), tongue (taste) and nostrils (smell). These are the data/

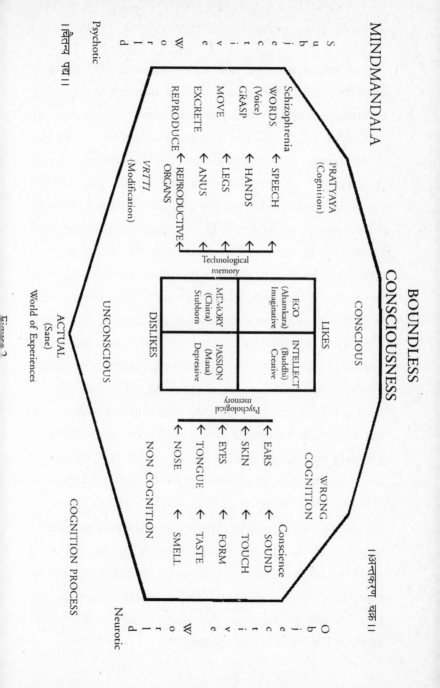

Figure 2

stimuli which is called *padarta* in Vedanta. The objective sensations reach the mind filtering through the existing technological and psychological memories, through the likes and dislikes and passions. The sensations, coloured by the conditionings of the mind are called *vishaya* or *vrtti*. When *vrtti* is provoked, every part of the mind is activated; in fact, the whole body undergoes a molecular change – physical, physiological, psychological. The moment a sensation impacts on the mind, memories are activated. The entire field of memory is scanned to get clues regarding the new sensation. For example, the object which caused the sensation, it could be perceived as a rope, a snake, a garland or a streak of water. The related information gathered from memory is then fed to *buddhi* (reasoning) which decides the identity of the object. The spontaneous reasoning may go like this: There was no rainfall for the past few days and so it cannot be a streak of water; there is no temple nearby and hence it cannot be a garland; there is no reason for a rope to be there so it has to be snake. The moment it is decided that it is a snake, the ego says, "I see a snake" and you react in a certain manner.

Ego plays a vital role in experiencing. Suppose your mind says that your neighbour is seeing a snake. Your reaction then would be different. Therefore, relating a sensation to you as an experience is very important. Once an experience is related to you, passions get aroused: "It is dangerous!" An immediate response is made and you run away.

The response to a stimulus is conveyed to a set of five instruments of action – speech, hands, legs, anus and reproductive organs. Any of them can get activated. In the above case when you are running away from the snake the response is conveyed to the legs. Suppose you see a fence and find that you cannot move further. Immediately a command is given to the hands to remove the fence. If that is not possible you shout (speech) for help. If that also fails, then you urinate (reproductive organ), or excrete (anus), out of fear. Thus the information coming to the mind is processed with reference to the ego standpoint. When passions are aroused, responses are created and implemented through motor organs. If you can remain awareful of this entire process, your life will undergo fundamental change and you will enjoy great mastery over your mind and sense organs.

Your response to sensation is known as experience. These experiences constitute your subjective world. Each one of your experiences depends upon your ego, *buddhi*, memory and so on, which means that the subjective world is different for different people. The objective world, of course, is the same for everybody. Handling the mind, therefore, is very difficult. Different people respond to the same sensation differently. In our earlier example, for instance, if the snake is seen by a snake charmer; instead of running away he will run to catch it! In creating an experience it is not only the objective world but your mind also which plays a role. The mind's contribution is conditioned by the objective world and your experience, the subjective world, is heavily influenced by the mind. Your action thus is a function of these two – the objective and the subjective. If you live exclusively in the subjective world you become a psychotic. On the other hand, if you are simply overwhelmed by the objective world you become a neurotic, a dysfunctional person, and will undoubtedly make a fool of yourself and a mess of your life. Your actual world is a mesh of both the objective and the subjective.

The next question is if everything is an interaction between the mind and the objective world, how does an interaction become an experience? Two ping-pong balls hitting each other do not create an experience for them. Experience – the mind-matter phenomenon – is for 'somebody'. There is somebody who knows the actual world, who knows the activities of the sense organs, who knows the activities of the mind, who knows even the knower (the one who experiences everything). The entire mechanism, the entire stage, is illuminated by the light of consciousness. The *vrtti*, the interaction between mind and matter, lighted up by consciousness becomes a *pratyaya* – knowledge, cognition and experience.

Consciousness illumining a thought modification (*vrtti*) becomes the 'conscious', and the conscious in time becomes the 'unconscious'. In sleep you are unconscious – meaning you are not conscious of thought modifications (*vrttis*). Consciousness illumines both the conscious and the unconscious – both the presence and absence of *vrittis* (thought modifications).

For total understading of the mind one must know the objective, the subjective and the actual world, and also the conscious and the unconscious, and lastly Consciousness. Dream is another dimension; it lies between the conscious and the unconscious. There are thus three states of the mind – sleep, dream and waking. Dream is an useful provision in the human psyche for taking away frustrations and fulfilling desires. Most of your impossible desires are fulfilled in dreams. In dream you create a private world of fulfilment. Whereas in sleep you are not conscious of anything. When you understand the whole process you become a person who knows, who has total wisdom. This is the mind you are operating. Mind is a result of all these operations. It is very dynamic. You have to bring into your mind the entire picture for a few days. In the *Gita* it is called '*Visvaroopa darsana*' – total vision, which is the same as the present day word 'vision'. When your vision is clear, then your mission also becomes clear. Picturising mind in its totality can become a mental *mandala*, *chakra*, or *yantra*. And that image can be useful in meditation, which leads you to total wisdom, the state which transcends the mind in all its manifestations. It is what the rishis called *turiya*, the fourth state, the state when the mind is absolutely quiet and you can connect with the 'total' mind or universal conscious. In Buddhist terminology it is known as No-mind, or nirvana.

Relationship

Our question is, how can one hold the vision of the whole while creatively working in the world?

This question is relevant because though the individual may be able to operate independently the full range and splendour of potential cannot be actualised in isolated action. Here individual-object relationship also is not enough. Individual-to-individual relationship alone can invoke the full potential of human beings.

The individual personality has got different levels – the body, mind and spirit. When you deal with a thing, only the physical level is involved. To understand another mind you have to understand your own mind. To understand someone's body you look outward, but to understand mind you look inward. Individual to individual interaction involves different levels.

Let us take the individual as a point intersection of a network of relationships – a point without any dimension in space and time (see Figure 3). That point can be indicated by the word "I". Whenever you say the word "I", you mean this point only. When you say "I am a father", it means that this 'point' relates to another person through the level of the body. Your relationships are always with reference to the body and mind. In your sleep you are not relating through the body-mind to

EXISTENCE AS A NETWORK

(The Whole Person)

1– *Pratyagatma*-Innermost person
   (Pure Consciousness)

2– Body-Mind

3– Family

4– Civil Society

5– Nature (Environment)

Jivatma (Empirical Self) = 1+2

Biological Self = 1+2+3

Social and Cultural Self = 1+2+3+4

Total Self (Complete Person) = 1+2+3+4+5

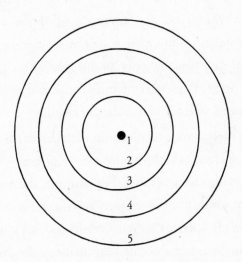

VALUES

For 1	→	Meditation
For 2	→	Discipline & (Satya Ahimsa) Austerity (Continence)
For 3	→	Love & Care
For 4	→	Respect & Trust
For 5	→	Worship & Adoration

Figure 3

another person, because you are not conscious. Therefore, it follows that in sleep you are not a father, since no emotions of a father arise in you. This point which has no space-time dimension (it is beyond the body, beyond the mind) is your real "I", the pure consciousness. The rest are all that you are conscious of – the body, the mind, space, time, etc. Therefore, you enjoy a possessive relationship with the body and mind, not an identity relationship. You *are* pure consciousness. Your first relationship is with the body-mind and their various functions which you are conscious of. Then you have a biological relationship with your family members. Ninety per cent of your personality is conditioned by the genetic and family heritage. Beyond the family is the civil society, which defines your economic and social personality.

Finally there is your relationship with nature, in which you live and operate, which determines to a large extent your psychosomatic characteristics. For example, the Arab and the desert. The uniformity, monotony and the unforgiving nature of the desert influence the Arab's worldview, his monotheistic fundamentalism and absolute submission to the divine will – "There is only one God, and no other God." Whereas Hindus living in a nature of abundance and diversity have become liberal and polytheistic – "As many people, so many gods." These are the various levels of interactions that the self or "I" enters into, such as with the ego, mind-body, family, civil society and nature. They collectively orchestrate your self-hood and self-worth. When you act all these come into action.

This is how you come to define yourself spiritually, psychologically, genetically, historically and culturally which creates your sense of Self, which in turn conditions your responses to situations. Unless the various levels of personality are integrated, living, which is a series of responses to challenges, becomes a cacophony – a medley of disharmonious noises.

The deepest level of the personality is known, in Vedanta, as the *pratyagatma*, the essential Self. The body-mind networking is called the *jivatman*, the empirical or historical self. *Pratyagatma* is the centre, *jivatma*, is the periphery. Most of us know only a centreless periphery. We are peripheral people, without any idea of the centre, because of which our selfhood is defined by what we *have* and not by what we *are*. For example the attitude that if you have money, you are on top of the world, if you don't you are nobody. Not only does the world feel that but you yourself have such an attitude about your worth. The world may call you by any name, but as long as you are not mesmerised by it, is okay. Remember that *jivatma* is just a collection of experiences. *Pratyagatma* is the centre. The first harmony to be achieved is on this level. The *pratyagatma* is free from space-time laws, good and bad deeds, and also from the operation of the law of causation. It is the field of infinite potential, the quantum soup. It is the field of God or *Ishvara*.

The body-mind level is subject to physical and ethical laws.

Knowing and living according to these laws helps you to live in harmony. The laws for the body are:

– Don't eat meat.

– Don't drink liquor.

– Don't smoke.

If you find it difficult to follow these instructions strictly, follow the Vedantic dictum of moderation, or "voluntary limits", in your lifestyle.

For the mind the laws advocated are:

– Speak truth (*Satyam*).

– Be respectful (*Ahimsa*).

Here also moderation (*mitatva*) is advocated because you cannot be very rigid about these rules, for rigidity is not desirable. Following these rules brings peace and harmony in the body-mind level.

According to our scriptures, you are allowed to tell a few lies provided the ultimate result is for the common good (e.g., in the Mahabharata battle, Lord Krishna asks Dharmaputra to say, "Aswathama is killed", while it was only a namesake elephant which was killed). There are several tests for the admissibility of such deviations from *satyam*. The second law of the mind is *ahimsa*, which means a healthy respect for others, for their uniqueness and selfworth. *Ahimsa* is not hurting people for your personal benefit. It is said, "do not hurt people on your way up, because on your way down you will meet them."

Family is an important aspect of your personality and selfhood. Family is the relationship between parents and children. Family relationships can be harmonised by developing respect for parents and love and care for offsprings. Recently in a seminar, we were trying to identify a core Indian value and all the participants agreed that the core value is 'respect for age'. Wisdom and age matter a lot to us. If you respect your elders, they bless you (*anugraha*). We know that our efforts alone are not enough for success; what makes our efforts (*prayatna*) fulfilled is the *anugraha* factor. No other country has such a concept. When you touch the feet of your elders before embarking on any activity, the success you achieve becomes more enjoyable. You create a synergy by respecting parents.

The third dimension of this network of relationships is the civil society, which comprises of relationships between teachers and pupils, employers and employees, and leaders and citizens. The teacher has to continuously learn. The primary function of a university is to create and disseminate knowledge, and to enlarge the intellectual assets of society. Trust between teacher and students is essential for the harmonious functioning of the university. So too trust between employer and the employees. The work places and factories are meant to create wealth, goods and services. Anything that hinders that goal is to be discouraged. Unfortunately, in a low trust society like ours citizens don't trust rulers and leaders. "*Sab chor hai*" is the general refrain. Nor does the leader feel secure enough to plan for the future, to take bold unpleasant decisions, and carry them out in a democratic framework. Thus, no gigantic tasks are undertaken. The society lives on an *ad hoc* basis, decisions are taken most arbitrarily. We need to cultivate a high level of trust between teacher-taught, employer-employee, and leader-citizen relationships for the efficient and creative functioning of our society. All this has to begin from yourself.

Finally, it is nature. Nature has been treated as an exploitable slave rather than as a caring mother. The result is that there are several ecological problems – global warming, acid rain, soil erosion, depleting forests, endangered animals, pollution, etc. We must learn to respect nature. The ancient rishis looked upon nature as life giving, a nourishing mother who was to be respected and worshipped for the bounty she provided for all.

Samudra vasane devi parvata stana mandale,
Vishnu patni nama tubhyam, pada sparsam kshamasva me

"O, Mother Earth! Consort of Lord Vishnu,
You are endowed with the nourishing mountains
and life supporting oceans,
I implore thee, pardon me for touching thee with my feet."

If we can revive this attitude to nature and such traditionally inherited habits and values of do's and don'ts (culture) we can build a high-trust, high-performance attitude in organisations at different levels (civil society, family, our own body-mind) and will be in a position to undertake gigantic tasks. In such a high-trust, well-integrated society, individuals grow fully integrated, capable of unleashing their full potentialities. In the *Bhagavad Gita* (XVII - 78) it is written:

Yatra yogesvara krishno,
Yatra partho dhanurdharah,
Tatra sri vijayo bhutir,
Dhruva nitir matir mama.

When Lord Krishna and Arjuna unite, three values emerge such as wealth (*Sri*), victory (*Vijaya*) and justice (*Niti*). These are the three values that we universally seek in life, and all other values can be reduced to these three values.

Understanding life in its wholeness will give you such power that you can create wealth, success and justice. We want to create a wealthy and competent society. All these are possible by living a wholesome spiritual life.

I have discussed certain laws of life and they are:

1. The law of infinite potentiality. This law says that you can achieve anything provided you believe that you are a field of infinite potentialities. Vedanta puts it very succinctly – *Shivoham* – I am Shiva.

2. Command thought and undertake activities which are commensurate with this belief. Desire and work then

185

become a means of invoking this potential. Desire is an important instrument of unfolding your potential. Desire rooted in self-awaress is the key to success and fulfillment. Desire has to be based on *dharma*, that is, on your uniqueness and your unique contribution to the social good. Your desire has to be in agreement with everybody else's *dharma*. *Dharma* has two dimensions, your own uniqueness, and the collective uniqueness of all other people. So entertain desires which are in agreement with your *dharma* and in harmony with the collective *dharma*. Cultivate such desires, discipline yourself and work diligently. You will enjoy such work because it is in tune with your nature, and it is in harmony with the collective destiny.

3. When you desire and work, the motivating attitude should be 'to give', because by giving you grow. The more you give, the more you will be given.

4. Give and receive. If you want to become competent, first give and then deserve what you need and expect. Trust and respect are to be given which will be received back a thousand-fold. Remember, trust begets trust.

Entertain desires and undertake activities according to your uniqueness, without losing sight of your own potentialities and the welfare of the world. Then you will find that your efforts are minimal. That is what is meant by the law of least effort. Step into the dance of nature, and you will find that nature will support you.

Affluence can be created by following the above laws, and by keeping in view the wholeness of existence. What you do according to your *dharma* is your *karma*, acting according to which you become proactive. Anything else makes you reactive.

These are some laws which you can follow. With this understanding work for wealth, success and justice. All these and more shall be yours.

4

Relationships

Life unfolds in terms of relationships and responses to relationships, which are kaleidoscopic in variety. Man is born into a network of relationships, defining for him his life situation. All our efforts to change relationships and situations result only in a tweedledee and tweedledum conundrum. Hence attention should be paid not only to changing situations and relationships, but also to the quality of responses we choose to interact with situations. It is our responses which give significance to a situation for us. Situations remaining the same, one can choose to be joyful, or miserable. We are responsible for our subjective happiness and sorrows, in the sense that we have the ability to choose our responses, which ultimately constitute our happiness or sorrow.

By consistent thought control, and deepening awareness, one should master the response patterns of the mind. This is possible through meditation and loving effort.

Interactions

Q 1:   Will organised labour and poor people accept the kind of change that you advocate?

Swamiji: Changes are taking place in Russia, in China, in Cuba. Ideologically blinkers are being removed to a considerable extent. Now it is only a kind of blabbering. You know, like a man who blabbers in his sleep. So a few leaders may blabber. A few followers too, because they have a stake in the ideology and that is their source of income. But I think an honest worker, if you explain things to him, will understand. What is important is producing wealth for all in our contry. Producing wealth is a co-operative effort. Capital, labour, land, technology everything must come together and therein lies your future. If you can explain to the working class properly, they are ready to co-operate in this country. And that is what we are going to do.

At least *sanyasis* will have to do that. Because people don't believe anybody else. When we speak to them, they know that we have no vested interest. So we are going to go around the country, tell the people. "You have to create wealth." Since wealth creation is a cooperative effort, different specialists must come together. Capital handling is no easy job. You may write a book on capital. I always tell that story. Marx wrote a book on capital. Then he went to his mother to borrow some capital.

So his mother asked: "Marx, I heard that you wrote a book on capital and you have no capital with you?" Therefore, handling capital is a very specialised job. We need specialists in all branches of economic activities. Even labour is not a simple thing now. Labour is knowledge. We call them knowledge-workers. Therefore we have to impress upon the people that our future lies in cooperation, not in hostility between capital and labour.

I do agree that in our country 60 per cent of the people are poor. So this kind of capital intensive, technology-oriented, global market and know-how – what impact will it have on the poor people? Of course that question is there. But there is no alternative other than creating wealth. That is the experience of all peoples and nations. Singapore, Indonesia, Taiwan, Hongkong, Japan – they all created wealth, then thought of distributing wealth. In our country we think of distributing wealth before we produce wealth. These things are to be explained to the people. Our people are intelligent – they will understand. We have to create an atmosphere for cooperative enterprises. The entrepreneur has to come to the forefront, not the bureaucrat. The bureaucrat has to gracefully leave the centre stage. He has to say that "I have done my work. Now I must work in the background." The entreprenur has to come. Capital has to come. Profit has to be respected. And every individual must be given the power to take decisions, economic decisions, in charting his own growth.

We have to have an entire new ethos for this country. Ideological divides are crumbling. And it is time we made concerted efforts. Our country is ready for it. The world is ready for it. Nor in the process are we going to blindly follow the Westerners, their capitalistic mode of production, and get into all the problems that they have created – the ecological problems, erosion of family values and psychological problems. If we can avoid all that, and create a new way of organising and producing wealth, that will be our contribution to the world.

Q 2:   What does your organisaton do practically in the field of management? And does it work?

Swamiji: I think you know this is a relatively new attempt made by us. Subramanian says it has helped him. He is a practicing manager. Vedanta and *Gita* thought has helped him. The next speaker, Mavlankar, is a person who practices this. So he will have a lot of experiences to share with you. And I admit we have no practical studies. This is the greatest lacuna in our discussion today – there is no documentation from practical experience. We have to address that problem. We are aware of that.

Q 3:   Swamiji, you said modern management concepts take man as "used less." Now there are theories which accept man as creative. Comment.

Swamiji: We are happy that modern management accepts that. Earlier they were not accepting it. Now our thoughts converge, that is why you invited me. Vedanta is concerned with the individual. Modern management also is concerned with the individual. Vedanta has something unique to say about man. And you want to know that. So I accept that modern management is coming to this theory that man is the focus.

Q 4:   If an efficient man is angry, he is *rajasic*. But *sattivc* people also become angry. How do you know a man's nature from his behaviour?

Swamiji: Very efficient people at the age of 40 have all kinds of physical problems – blood pressure, sugar and stomach ulcers. They have no self-control. They want to be quiet but because of various pressures, they are angry. Later they say, "I am sorry." And everybody knows that; that is their nature. Or they have stomach ulcers, heart problems – haven't you seen such efficient people? Those are *rajasic* person. A *sattvic* person will not have that problem. Because he is quiet. He doesn't take anything upon himself. A top-level manager should be like that. Quiet and efficient, very alert. Because when you are agitated, you are not alert and your decisions become impulsive.

You should know whom you are dealing with. To an extremely *tamasic* person you may have to show anger. Like Rama did. When you get angry, don't become anger. You show anger. He came to Varuna. Varuna was a *tamasic* person –

lying down all the time under water. Rama had to show anger. Then Varuna appeared. Rama said, "Doesn't matter, get my work done." Anger must be shown. '*Krodh karna hai, hona nahi.*'

You alone know whether anger has gone into your system or whether you are using it merely as a weapon. Others may not know. Others will know later – after two or three years, when you have the first heart attack, they will realise you have been suffering within.

Q 5: Swamiji you said latent qualities in man die out without manifesting in his lifetime. In India now, as a matter of fact, we have got very good people in every field but we are not able to come to the forefront in any field whatsoever, especially in the international field. That is because there is no proper environment for the children to develop so that they can bring out their latent qualities. Also, we can say that we are more in *tamasic* energy. Have you any practical suggestions to give so that we can bring more people to *rajasa* rather than keep them in *tamasa*?

Swamiji: That is why I said you must have national goals. Define your national goals. Like America has a national goal. They want to remain a superpower. They always wanted to be a superpower. Every child knows that. Japan has got a national goal – export, otherwise perish. It is in their blood. We have no national goal at all. So somebody has to define a national goal by which you can galvanise this *tamasic* energy into *rajasic* energy. First, from *tamas* to *rajas*. Somebody has to do that. Political leadership is not able to do that. They are very confused.

Therefore, thinkers are needed. They have to sit together and national goals have to be discussed and decided. What should be the national goal? The national goal should be spiritually higher rather than simply surviving as a chaotic democracy. Our national goal should be to command world attention. And India can do that according to the latest study about the 21st century. But we are still thinking in terms of the 14th and the 18th centuries.

So how should we behave? What are the forces which are going to operate in the 21st century? And where will be our place in it? Taking all these into consideration, we should define our national goals, communicate them to the people, and reform our educational system in the process. Either the government has to do it or individuals have to start. We are doing it our own way. Some technique has to be used to whip up *tamasic* people into *rajas*. And then from *rajas* to *sattva*, and finally from *sattva* to *sattvatita*. Your growth is endless.

At this crucial juncture, for us *rajas* is more important because you cannot move straight from *tamas* to *sattva* even if you want to. Very few people can move directly from *tamas* to *sattva*. Therefore, first we have to move people from *tamas* to *rajas* – to egoistic activity. You must develop a national ego just as America is doing. They fought a war in Kuwait. That is the expression of their national ego. They fought it and they won it, the mother of all battles. America could do that. More recently, after the attack on the World Trade Centre on 11 September 2001, they launched a massive strike against the Taliban whom they held responsible. Their national interest was involved. They could clearly define it, and work accordingly.

We, on the other hand, don't know what are our interests then how can we know how to go about securing them? So a lot of thinking has to go into that. The only certainty is that India can do it. Everybody else knows it too – that say the 21st century belongs to India. But are we prepared for it? This is the question. Are we prepared mentally, emotionally and psychologically?

Q 6:   Is the quality of a swami? *Sattva* or *rajas*?

Swamiji: A swami is a transcendental person – beyond *sattva*. He is a person who observes everything, identified with nothing. For a swami, disidentification is the key. He must have moved from *tamas* to *rajas* to *sattva* and then beyond. I would call him a transcendental leader. He creates and leaves his creation behind and goes ahead. That is the quality of a swami. Swami means a master.

Q 7:   Is American culture one of consumerism? They have progressed even though they, like us, are not Self-centred. What is the reason for their success?

Swamiji: Their culture is based on individual freedom. Of course they don't have the complete picture of the individual. Their culture is based on individual choices. If you read the American Constitution these are natural rights – the right to life, liberty and the pursuit of happiness. The individual and his choices are the focus of concern. Government only organises individual choices. So they are able to stimulate individual initiative in their society. That is their success.

But then there is failure also; for instance violence. There the individual is only an emotional individual, the physical individual, the consumerist individual. In America every year 50,000 people die in gun-battles alone, which was the number of people lost in the entire Vietnam war. Their concept of happiness is enjoyment – physical enjoyment – resulting in disintegration of the family, violence and madness. According to a recent survey, 60 per cent of Americans are crazy.

We people are at least sober. Look at the amount of tolerance in our society. As we drive, we see somebody cutting a coconut from a wayside coconut tree. And all the vehicles stop there to watch that man cut the coconut. In any other country they would have gone ahead, they wouldn't have bothered. And if the coconut falls on their heads, they will file a suit against the offender. And the complainant will get 10 million dollars compensation. All for one coconut!

Their's is a totally different system. Here we have infinite tolerance. Tolerance is a great quality. But tolerance has become counter-productive. Everything is tolerated! Wisdom means striking a balance. This is a matter for sagacious leadership. The sagacity of the leader, an individual, lies in defining goals, and attaining them, in working together. So we should sit and discuss matters. It takes practice also. Over a period of time, we have to develop that national will. The political leadership and thinkers should be doing this but we can also contribute to that dialogue.

Q 8: You said we have to define national goals for a better India. I just heard somebody asking you for a practical suggestion for today's world but you just passed the buck back to him. Why don't you suggest a remedy?

Swamiji: No, I didn't do that. I said you cooperate with us. We will sit together. You didn't hear me properly. I said instead of asking me let us sit together. So what does that mean? Together we will sit down. All of us will have to sit together. You will put a question to me. I will put a question to you. Together we will find answers. Everybody should take the responsibility. Let us not pass responsibility. If nobody else is taking responsibility, you must take it. You should not sit down there and say, "Everybody is passing the buck, so let me also pass the buck." Somebody has to take it up. Either me, or you, or somebody else.

And we can do it. Every creative idea begins as an invisible impulse. Then it grows and gains momentum. You don't know the power of thought.

Q 9:   According to medical science, people differ in capacities whereas Vedanta says infinite power is within you. How do you reconcile that?

Swamiji: Medical science deals only with the physico-psycho complex which is a combination of *sattva*, *rajas* and *tamas*. On this level every individual is different. You are different from me on the body-mind level. But we are all one on the spiritual level – which is beauty, happiness, and intelligence. So on that level we are one. We have to draw from that level and that is possible when you become integrated on the physico-psycho level. That is how Vedanta conceives it.

If you bring destiny into that, then there is no scope for initiative. How do I know what you are destined for? So let us work. Let us work and see what we are destined for. When the individual works with this attitude, Vedanta says it is possible right here and now – "*Adyaiva atraiva ihaiva*" – to achieve. So why should we deny that possibility? Let us try. Let us not bring in thoughts of pessimism and cynicism into work. Let us work with enthusiasm.

Q 10:   What does unfolding your potential mean?
Swamiji: Unfolding an individual's potential means to work

on his *sattva, rajas, tamas* complex, his programming. Everyone has a given programming. And according to that programming, he must find work. His work must also be in tune with the *samasthi* – the totality. It must be in tune with national goals because no individual can work independently. That is where the *yajna* concept arises. So you must find your full potential just as a stick finds its full potential when it is tied together in a bundle. The individual has to work as a team, as part of a nation, may be as part of the world. In the process, the individual unfolds his glory. The individual can do that. It is all tied together.

The individual has got two dimensions – spiritual, which is the dimension of beauty, power, intelligence, and of the personality or character traits – *sattva, raja* and *tamas*. When you work, you can work as a combination of *sattva, raja* and *tamas*. You cannot work as a spirit. So the unfoldment of *sattva, raja* and *tamas* through your work becomes a means of unfolding your spirit. It is something like when a flower opens its petals, there is a physical act and through that is the manifestation of beauty. In the same way, when you work, your inner beauty, inner spirit which is invisible, manifests itself.

Q 11: The mind is connected with food. How is the mind connected with body economics?

Swamiji: The essence of the food that you eat helps the mind to function – the *sattvic* aspect of that essence remains as the

201

mind. The body is only a vehicle for expressing the mind. And the body also is sustained by food. When you don't eat food, the mind does not disappear. It is there. The mind has no vehicle to express, because of weakness. Again when you eat food, the mind manifests itself. All that you have learnt again manifests itself.

Q 12: We have a body and mind. Is enlightenment a state of mind? Is realisation within the mind?

Swamiji: Strictly speaking, enlightenment is not a state of mind. It is a state of consciousness where the mind has awakened to higher possibilities. But there remains a sort of mind called *badhita mana* by which you are able to interact with the world. An enlightened person also moves about in the world. He has also got a sort of mind, but not the old mind. It is a very enriched mind.

Realisation is beyond the mind, not within the mind. The mind is limited. Realisation is discovering yourself as other than the mind. Let me put it this way. When you are driving a car you know yourself as other than the car and the handling of the car. You do not identify with the car. So handling your body with your mind, you stand apart as a separate being. That is realisation.

Q 13: Abraham Maslov referred to self-actualisation, how do you view it?

Swamiji: It is open to discussion. I don't know whether he understood what he said or all the possibilities of those words. Self-actualisation is a state where you do what you want to. Meaning, you are not under the pressure of society, economic, social, or ego needs. You can just be and do what you want to. This is self-actualisation. For example, when a person reaches the top of his organisation he retires or entrusts the job to his subordinates and starts learning music, gardening, *bonsai*, attends spiritual classes or visits *ashrams*, (he always wanted to do a little meditation and all that), or play with his grandchildren. It is a time when you have the inner-leisure and inner-richness to do what you want to do. This state of mind is self-realisation.

Q 14: Self-actualisation is important. But the individual may not have the opportunity for self-actualisation due to other constraints.

Swamiji: That is the limitation of our present level of economic progress. The more our economy progresses, the more individuals will get opportunities to express themselves better. There seems to be a historical constraint in self-actualisation. So perhaps society has to organise itself better and progress to a level where every individual can express himself.

Modern managers optimise – they put resources to optimum use. That is why there will always be some disagreement and dissatisfaction in the organisation. Bhagavan says in the *Gita*, there is no *karma* which is defect-free (*Bhagavad Gita*, Ch. XVIII-48): "*Sarvarmbha hi doshena dhumenagni rivavrta*". There is no situation where a particular decision particular placement, a particular training is perfect. There will always be some deficiency in all the initiatives that you take. It cannot be otherwise.

We are not in a position to organise society to place every individual in the right position. We have not developed that economic efficiency. But individual happiness does not depend upon that. Individual happiness is unrelated to situations. You have to work to the best of your ability, with detachment. To be a happy person you don't have to have an evolved society but to get the right placement, society must grow.

Q 15:   Swamiji, you describe effectiveness as the quality necessary to work as a team. And as far as I understand, from your talk, the global market is opened for leaders. You yourself are addressing the three to five per cent of the people – the leaders. It is true that competitiveness is the quality necessary for the leaders. Does the quality of effectiveness pertain to the leader or to the middle level manager? Because if one wants to be a leader, according to His Holiness, organisational interests are secondary. The leader should have global interests. Hence can a leader be effective and competitive at the same time?

Swamiji: Effectiveness and competitiveness go together – they are great leadership qualities along with innovativeness. Without working as a team, the leader will not be able to translate his ideas into practice. He has to inspire people, communicate with them, nourish them by his ideas, and be nourished in turn by their responses. A leader creates his own organisation. The structure of his organisation will be loose and chaotic, non-hierarchical. The organisation will twist and bend, and be sensitive to all creative ideas. The leader will inspire leadership in others in his relentless pursuit of excellence. An organisation is only a device, a means, not the end in itself. He will not be loyal to an organisation which fails to inspire the best in him, an organisation which fails to help him pursue excellence and explore the limits of his potential. An obese, ponderous organisation cannot contain him. Only a lean and mean organisation with global interests can inspire him. When an organisation shies away from global competition and withdraws into its narrow organisational interest, it stagnates. And stagnant water breeds only worms. But a leader cannot compete alone; he has to carry the whole team with him – like in a football match, or in an army operation.

Q 16:   Swamiji, you remarked that 90 per cent of man's personality is the unconscious. Do you think that the whole history of human civilisation is just an expression of the collective unconscious?

Swamiji: Collective unconscious is a fluid concept. It causes civilisation, and in turn is influenced by civilisation. It is not a monotonous, pre-destined unfoldment but a mutually determined, creative dynamic. And the unconscious is not the ultimate. The Self is the ultimate; the tension, and the resultant dynamic movement caused by that tension between the conscious and the unconscious, civilisation and nature, is the vehicle for the Self to express itself in myriad forms.

Q 17: In your talk, Swamiji, you emphasised the Capitalist mode of economic development, where wealth is God. Is it not against our ancient value system where *artha* comes only after *dharma*? Do you think that the Capitalist mode of development and one's spiritual development are complementary?

Swamiji: Spiritual well-being and material welfare are complementary. Capitalism creates wealth. And wealth is God. What is wealth? It is utility; it is the power to satisfy human needs. It is the creative power of God manifested as ideas, effort and products. If consumption causes individual and ecological degradation, it is not the fault of wealth but the stupidity of the human mind. We have to put limits on consumption. *Dharma* is an order of society where nobody is exploited, and everybody is respected and free; where one individual's freedom is not opposed to his neighbour's freedom. A *dharmic* situation is necessary for the creation of genuine wealth for the country, where people can freely unfold themselves. The Capitalist mode of development is also an evolving concept. Presently it means development through savings and capital. Lately it also has come to mean development by consumption, even by borrowing. What is important is creation of wealth, which means ideas, and translating them into useful products which requires self-exploration and team work, getting along with people and upgrading the quality of the work force.

Q 18: I don't quite understand when you say that development has lately come to mean development by consumption, even by borrowing.

How can one develop if one consumes more? Are not consumption and development antagonistic concepts? Is it not a reiterative statement of Charvakan hedonism?

Swamiji: The Capitalist mode of development is driven by mass consumption, which necessitates mass production, resulting in more quality goods at cheaper prices. The SONY company tries to increases its profits not by selling their 'walkman' at higher and higher prices to fewer and fewer people, but by selling it at lower and lower prices to more and more people. They use the latest technology to produce large volumes of the same goods. The same customer cannot consume all the 'walkmans' that SONY produces and hence they have to find new consumers, conquer new markets, offer new incentives to sell their products to more and more people. Thus, in the Capitalist mode of production there is no concentration of consumption by a few households but rather there is mass distribution. The Birlas, Ambanis, Tatas, use the same brand and same number of televisions, cars, washing machines, cooking ranges as any other ordinary middle-class family. When consumption becomes mass-based, economic activity becomes more democratic. In America, an income of $ 15000 a year is considered to be below the poverty line – that is one who earns Rs 4.5 lakh a year is poor! In India he is super rich. Capitalism has been much more effective in producing wealth, equitably distributing the wealth, and reducing the income differential among the upper and lower strata of society than any totalitarian or communist state. A drop in consumption of society and demand affects production, which affects wages, and which in turn affects further demand causing a vicious circle and results in economic depression. So Capitalist economies encourage the individual to borrow and consume, and pay gradually. Thus you get loans for virtually anything – buying cars, houses, etc. That is what I meant by development by consumption. It does not mean idle indulgences in drinks, sex, music, and dance but rather building a comfortable, good life for the citizens of a society or a country. In the common perception mass consumption has become a metaphor for an idle, non-creative, dissipating, indulgent lifestyle but the original Hedonists and Epicureans or (Charvakas) were not like that. They believed that the joys of this world were real and the other world is only a dream. They asked people to discipline and train themselves to enjoy the world to the hilt, including sexual enjoyment. *Kamasutra* is a product of this school.

Q 19:   Swamiji, you remarked that "God-realisation is Goal realisation." Is God a goal to be realised? If at all God-realisation is goal-realisation, what kind of a goal is it – economic, religious, ethical, social or spiritual?

Swamiji: When we say God-realisation is goal-realisation we don't mean that God is separate from us to be realised, in time, in space, or a separate object to be possessed, exploited and indulged in. On the contrary, it is like a seed flowering. Under the earth, it dreamed of light and the sun, it wanted to touch the stars. It sprouted, stretched its branches, it heaved itself through numberless shoots, leaves and twigs and finally it flowered. Aiming at the sun it discovered itself in the flowers. When you jump higher and longer, and run faster, you are experiencing your inner being. The unfoldment of Self is God. What you have achieved outwardly is nothing. What you have experienced inwardly is everything. In that attitude you never rest with one achievement; you never gloat over one success. You leave that behind, you forget the past and march ahead. Others write history, you create history.

Q 20: Swamiji, how can one be a leader if he is not loyal to his organisation? You say that the top-level manager need not be loyal to a particular organisation; what is important for him is his satisfaction and rewards. If that is his attitude, how can an organisation progress? If the organisation as a whole does not progress, then in what terms can we talk about economic development? Is economic development based on the loyalty of the manager to his own interests, or to the interests of the organisation? When we say "You are the leader", it is the organisation represented by you that is the leader. In the market, leadership or competitiveness relate to the product of the company – one is a leader because of the back-up of his company. Hence, should the manager stay with the ups and downs of his company, or should he quit and go for looking greener pastures?

Swamiji: A leader's satisfaction is not in external rewards, but an organisation's relevance, efficiency and success is measured by its capacity to reward its employees competitively. For the same job, measured in terms of time and expertise, if one organisation pays Rs. 100 and another Rs. 1,000, either the first organisation is non-economic, or the employee is mediocre, because of which productivity suffers and that itself results in low profits and low wages. A good leader will whip the organisation and the employees, in the same way a good rider whips the horse in a race to get supreme performance. And still if the organisation does not respond, he is not a necrophile to live with a corpse, or a neurotic martyr to stay in a gutted house. Only mediocre people work in such organisations. It is also true that no leader can achieve without an organisation. It is also true that no leader can achieve with a dysfunctional terminally ill organisation. Either he cures it or he quits it. Loyalty should not be an excuse for inefficiency, neither on the part of the employee nor of the organisation.

Q 21: You said "Creativity cannot be a collective product." It is true that the first glimmer of a creative impulse arises in the individual's mind. But earlier, in another talk, you had described *yajna* as a collective effort for a creative production. How do you distinguish between the creativity of the individual mind and that of the collective mind? Is there any antagonism between the two statements made by you? How do you define the creative endeavour of '*palazhy manthanam*? Was it not a collective product?

Swamiji: In the creation of ideas, vision and inventions it is the individual mind which plays the decisive role. The group can work on a hint, or a lead, or on a specific project. But it is only an individual who can think unstructured, bold, chaotic, new thoughts. A team can help an individual in making the idea or vision and also thereafter in converting that idea into a product and marketing it. A group can prod the individual and inspire him. Therefore, the team should never discourage the individual initiative. The Communists failed in all creative fields with their collective approach. The Japanese are not good inventors but are only efficient adaptors in converting an idea into a product. The *yajna* concept is not just a team concept. It inspires each individual to bring out his best and then organise that inspired energy, and offer that synergy to the altar of higher and higher achievements. The ultimate flame of creativity blazes in the individual mind. The team comes before and after it. The team can convert an idea into reality, but the individual alone can create the idea. The team can also create an environment for individuals to create visions. In the myth of the churning of the milky ocean, Vishnu gave the idea; the *devas* and *asuras* came together and worked as a team to implement the idea. The flaming tip of the collective mind is the individual mind – the genius of the leader.

Q 22:   Pujya Swamiji, you speak of global competitiveness and setting targets higher and higher. But I, as a manager, can compete only from the realm of my organisation. I have to safeguard the interests and standards set by my organisation. I cannot forsake them just to be a leader. Would you say then, that the individual will be limited by smaller initiatives? In the world of global competitiveness can an individual be a leader? It seems only companies and corporations can be leaders!

Swamiji: Competitiveness is global competitiveness because the world economic space is one. You and your company will be wiped out sooner than later if you don't develop that competitiveness. So a competitive manager's job is to make his company globally competitive. To do that one need not grow to the size of an IBM or General Motors, or a SONY. In fact they are flabby and middle-aged and their smaller, lean and mean competitors always outwit them in the market. They survive just because of their size. Competitiveness is utilising your strengths and weaknesses in such a manner that you go on growing and increasing your profit. If you think that your competitive worth suits only the organisation in which you work, then continue there in the same way. If you think you can do more, restructure your organisation. If the organisation is unresponsive leave it if you have guts, or suffer your guts out. Don't hide your incompetence behind pithless ideologies like loyalty. True loyalty is your feeling towards one who challenges the best in you. That corporation becomes a leader which is managed by first class leadership manpower. After all corporations are made up of people!

Q 23:   The *Bhagavad Gita* is known as a spiritual text. Swamiji, how can you say that economic problems can be solved by an unde⋯nding of the *Gita*?

Swamiji: Spiritual problems are not divorced from economic problems. All aspects of human existence are inter-related. The *Gita* advocates the pursuit of four Purusharthas – *dharma, artha, kama* and *moksha* – "*Dharmavirudho bhuteshu kamosmi bharatarshaba.*" "Desire which does not transgress *dharma* is indeed divine," says the *Gita*. Only a spiritually rooted person can perform efficiently in this world. Bhagavan inspired Arjuna to undertake a worldly activity through the teaching of the *Gita*. The vision and values of the *Gita* show us a path of harmonising economic activities with spiritual pursuits. God and man together create prosperity, success, welfare and justice. To hold that our worldly existence and struggles have nothing to do with spirituality and *vice versa* is due to a partial view of spirituality. Spiritual understanding helps one to look at the economic problems much more deeply and offer new solutions. Spiritual rootedness makes man more creative and effective. Therefore, the *Gita,* being a spiritual text, addresses the totality of life of which economics is a part.

Q 24:   Can you elaborate on the statement "Goal-realisation is God realisation"?

Swamiji: God realisation is not a static one-time event frozen in the past. According to Vedanta, God realisation is Self-realisation; the Self being all inclusive and dynamically creative in its fullness. Self-realisation cannot be an experience divorced from daily living. In fact Self-realisation is a continuous experience of one's infinitude in the midst of all worldly activities. When we set a goal and strive towards its fulfilment, the energies that unfold and the beauty that manifests in that pursuit is a manifestation of the infinite Self. For the ignorant and the egoistic, work is a source of conflict and dissipation. For the self-rooted, work is a source of unfolding his inner spirit. For the seeker work is a means of purifying his mind. By setting the goals higher and higher, one goes deeper and deeper exploding a series of energies, experiencing God as continuous bliss in the realisation of goals. For an ordinary egoistic person, goal-realisation is acquiring something from outside for ego gratification. But for a spiritual person goal-realisation is a means of drawing from his inner spiritual source. The first goal-realisation is an aggrandisement – *samsara*. The second goal-realisation is a self-giving experience – *sanayasa*.

Q 25: Swamiji, how can we relate economic development with psychological forces?

Swamiji: Mind is the real worker. Mind is the real consumer, people the resource. Materials, money and machines come second. Motivating people to work is the main economic problem. Therefore economic development is intimately related to psychological forces.

Q 26:   Swamiji, you said that for innovativeness one has to move into the Self. What is the procedure?

Swamiji: When I use the word Self, I mean all that complex oceanic inter-related dimension of human existence which is beyond the superficial individual mind, and is beyond the unconscious. All ideas are embedded there like diamonds and gold nuggets in the bowels of the earth. Ideas spring forth from the depth of the mind as a response to challenges. To move within-ward, one needs the quality of silent meditation, great empathy and sensitivity to various forces that are acting in the human world, and also a capacity for unstructured meshing of diverse intellectual disciplines. Only then can we remain close to the inner rumbling in the core of life.

Q 27:   Swamiji, you explain the Self as the all-pervading, non-reacting, witness consciousness. How can I improve effectiveness by abiding in the Self?

Swamiji: Effectiveness is expressed as the capacity of getting work done by a team of knowledge workers. Personal efficiency alone is not sufficient for effectiveness, though personal efficiency is an important input in effectiveness. For effectiveness, one must have the mental agility, clarity of goal, confidence, and humility to communicate, to understand and to get along with others. For that one should have control over the ego and egoistic weaknesses such as anger, jealousy, complexes, fear of failure and sudden outbursts. One should also develop the capacity to respect and integrate dissimilar views to one's plan of action. By abiding in the Self one is able to dis-identify with the body-mind personality as a part of cosmic machine-like wheels in wheels. That kind of a vision helps one to become modest about oneself and respectful towards others, which will increase one's effectiveness. In effectiveness the emphasis is on seeing oneself as part of a complex whole.

Q 28:   Swamiji, is not envy, anxiety for result, etc., part and parcel of competitiveness?

Swamiji: When you try to compete with another person and his standards, you are driven by jealousy, anger and anxiety. Then your success remains on the level of mediocrity. That kind of competitiveness is only *matsaryabuddhi* or spiteful competition. But when you set zero-defect standards yourself, you are in combat with your own inefficiencies; you stretch to know your own limits. Then you are a real competitor and you excel in your field without undergoing the self defeating indignities of jealousy and anxiety. Perhaps the approximate Sanskrit words to express the second type of competitiveness are *dakshatva* (efficiency), *kusalata* (competition for excellence), *appramadattva* (faultless efficiency). In other words, an incessant pursuit of excellence. Arjuna used to practice whole nights to know the sheer joy of excellence in archery. That is the kind of competitiveness that we advocate, from excellence to excellence.

Radio Interview

Interviewer: Today when India is opening its economy in the world market, Swamiji, what do you think is the place of spirituality in the style of Indian management?

Swamiji: For the creation of wealth for the country, we need a scientific method. And that scientific method is management. And in the modern world, management people are thinking of the individual. How to motivate the individual. How to inspire the individual. The Indian spiritual tradition also talks about the individual, his different dimensions, his integrity. Indian tradition talks about work culture, the *yajna* spirit, so on and so forth. So, I think that the Indian tradition and Indian values have a great role to play in formulating a new management ethos for our country.

Interviewer: You said Indian tradition speaks about the *yajna* spirit. How do you relate it with work?

Swamiji: *Yajna* means collective, dedicated work. Getting along with people and getting work done through them is the true spirit of *yajna* and work culture. If we educate people about our tradition, the *yajna* spirit, perhaps we will be able to create a new work culture in this country.

Interviewer: There is an opinion that Indian managers lack work culture. Swamiji, how would you comment on this evaluation?

Swamiji: I don't believe so. It is not the Indian manager who lacks work culture. There is a general environment of laziness and postponement, of passing the buck, in this country. The poor Indian manager becomes a victim of the system. Therefore, unless we get the right kind of leadership – political leadership and intellectual leadership – we will not be able to change the general tenor of people in this country. But once the general tenor of thinking changes, then every manager will respond to the changed situation.

Interviewer: If we have to change the general tenor of work culture, where should we begin?

Swamiji: We should begin with the leadership. As it is said in the *Bhagavad Gita* (*Gita*, III-21): "*Yadyadacarati sreshtah tattadeva etarojanah.*" So the change should begin from the leader and percolate downward. Once we had a great leader, Gandhiji. His word was law. And all the other leaders followed him. The glory of Gandhiji got projected onto the other leaders, and in turn the masses followed Gandhiji. We need such a leadership that can define our national goals and communicate those goals to people and inspire the whole population to undertake great national tasks. And it must begin from the leader.

Interviewer: You spoke about leaders and about them communicating ideas to workers. But it is often said today that there is an antagonism between the leader-class, or the manager-class, and the trade union workers. How does the leader or manager relate with workers?

Swamiji: Right. There is an atmosphere of confrontation, antagonism between the labourer, the Capitalists and the organisation. Therefore we have to tell the workers, "You have to work." You have to tell the managers, "You have to make the workers feel they belong to the organisation." When such a spirit of belongingness comes, the workers will understand. People will like co-ordinated activity.

Interviewer: It is generally believed that there is a lack of motivation in the group of workers. How can the workers be motivated?

Swamiji: Workers will need explanations. You must tell them that by working hard they are going to be benefited. If they don't work hard, the managerial class is not affected. They will get their salary because they are in the commanding positions of the economy. So the ultimate sufferer will be

221

the working class. They are the ones who sweat under the sun. Still 50 per cent of the population in India lives below the poverty line. So unless we create national wealth, we cannot think of sharing the wealth. And creating wealth means that every section of society must work together. Then alone can wealth be created. And without wealth, talking about distribution of wealth will not be feasible. It will be a foolish idea.

Interviewer: Swamiji, in your lectures on management, you often refer to the significance of positive thinking and creative work. How do you define positive thinking?

Swamiji: Positive thinking is a feeling, individual and collective, that "We can do." Generally the question arises that India is a backward country, or if you open the doors of our country we will not be able to compete with the foreign companies and they will swallow us up. I don't share that idea. We can compete with the multinationals and we can have our own place in the community of nations provided we think we can – as an individual, as a nation, as a people. That kind of a positive thinking is necessary in our country. And we have done great tasks in the past; we fought a non-violent war for independence and got our freedom. And we can do it again to compete in the world market and create a slot for ourselves in the world.

Interviewer: You spoke about a work culture. Today in India we see that we often miss the team-building or the ability of a group of workers to work as a team. So how do you comment on this observation?

Swamiji: We have to explain to our people, as I told you before, what should be the national goals, the organisational goals, the company's goals, and how this particular individual stands to benefit from the fulfilment of those goals. If has not been explained properly to the individual, that he stands to benefit, then he will turn his face against it. Therefore, it is very important that we explain it to them. Let everybody feel that they belong to this country and the glory of this country will in turn be their glory. And in that glorious work of recreating the country, reinventing our own inner source, everybody has to participate.

Interviewer: So Swamiji, can we say that self-realisation has an important role in the management of the whole lifestyle?

Swamiji: Yes. When we say, "You create wealth," what we

mean is that in the process of creating wealth you are discovering your inner potential. When I take a piece of stone and chip off the edges and produce a beautiful idol out of it, I am, in fact, unfolding my soul in that stone. That work of creation is an experience of self-discovery for me. So we have to make these managers understand that their self-discovery, their self-unfoldment, depends upon creative, co-operative, dedicated work. That is the only way to success and fulfilment in life.

Interviewer: Swamiji, to come to the final question. What is your message to the world of management?

Swamiji: The world of Indian management! Indian managers who have been entrusted with the task of creating wealth in this country! The government has abdicated their responsibilities. They say we will just govern, we will just co-ordinate, you intelligentsia come up, motivate the people. To those managers my message is work together and create wealth for this poor country. And once you create wealth, then you can think of distribution. So inspire the people to come together, to dream big and then create wealth for us. That is my final message to the world of Indian management.

Arise! Awake! Realise!

His Holiness Swami Bodhananda
his work and mission

Swami Bodhananda is a renowned Vedanta seer and scholar, teaching Vedanta and meditation for the last twenty years. He is an effective public speaker, classroom teacher as well as a private counsellor. Swamiji is a mystic with spiritual and occult powers to heal both the body and the mind. With a great grasp of the psyche of modern man, born of his lively interest in the day-to-day affairs of people, nations and societies, supplemented by his wide reading and honed by his spiritual practices, Swamiji is considered a unique religious master. His presence and words are a truly self-transforming experience. He feels our hearts, knows our inner thoughts, he touches our being and speaks the language of love. His teaching unfolds a vision which enriches and empowers our lives.

Swami Bodhananda wandered for several years in the Himalayas in search of masters and truth. During this time, he mastered Vedanta, meditation, Vedic cosmology, and human psychology.

Swamiji has devised various meditation techniques, blending Kundalini yoga and modern psychological discoveries in the background of Vedantic insights. His contributions in the field of the development of human potential are significant.

In the past, Swamiji has also served as the Chief Acharya of a residential academy for the training of Vedantic teachers.

His publication, *The Gita and Management*, is widely read by management practitioners and he is often invited to speak at management seminars in various parts of India. His other books include *Rishi Vision, Meditation - The Awakening of Inner Powers* and *Happiness Unlimited: Self-Unfoldment in an Interactive World.*

Swamiji is the founder chairman of the following organisations:

1   Sambodh Foundation, New Delhi, India

2   The Sambodh Society Inc., Los Angeles, USA

3   Bodhananda Research Foundation for Management and Leadership Studies, (BRFML), Thiruvananthapuram, India.

Swami Bodhananda is also the spiritual head of Bodhananda Seva Societies of Kerala and Bangalore. For further details contact:

1   **Sambodh Foundation**
     K-11 Kailash Colony
     New Delhi 110 048
     Tel 2628 9247
     Email: swami2@ndf.vsnl.net.in

2 **The Sambodh Society Inc.**
Trustee: Ruth Harring
1826 Charter Avenue
Portage MI 49024
Tel 269-327-3774
Email: indialink@worldnet.att.net

Or

C/o Uma Deperalta
7002 N-LA Presa Drive
San Gabriel CA-91775, USA.
Tel. : 626 –292-6883
Fax: 626-3077369

3 **Bodhananda Research Foundation**
for Management & Leadership Studies
Bodhananda Kendra
Kaldy-Karamana
Thiruvananthapuram, Kerala
Pin : 695002
Tel. : 2433084, 2448843.
email: tvm_brfmldns@sancharnet.in
visit websites: www.sambodh.com
                    www.sambodh.org